accepting JOY

a novel

Todd F. Cope

CFI

Springville, Utah

ISBN 13: 978-1-55517-962-5
ISBN 10: 1-55517-962-2

Published by CFI, an imprint of Cedar Fort, Inc., 2373 W. 700 S., Springville, UT, 84663
Distributed by Cedar Fort, Inc. www.cedarfort.com

LIBRARY OF CONGRESS CATALOGING-IN-PUBLICATION DATA

   Cope, Todd F.
   Accepting joy / by Todd F. Cope.
      p. cm.
   ISBN 1-55517-962-2 (acid-free paper)
   1. Religious fiction. I. Title.

   PS3603.O64A65 2007
   813'.6--dc22

                                    2006029164

Cover design by Nicole Williams
Cover design © 2006 by Lyle Mortimer
Printed in the United States of America

10 9 8 7 6 5 4 3 2 1

Printed on acid-free paper

accepting ✺ JOY

a novel

*To Victoria Ann Durfey and Jacqueline Kreiner,
whose lives inspired the Joy in this story.*

acknowledgments

I would like to thank Joseph Dinkins, MD, and Jeffery Juchau, MD, for acting as valuable resources in my research. Also to my nieces, Rebecca Merrill Durphey and Katherine Merrill Kreiner, thank you for your examples as mothers and for sharing your daughters with all of us.

chapter ✿ ONE

"I'll be right back," Rachel said to Mary as she stood and left the room to answer the ringing telephone.

"I'll still be here," her sister replied as she continued sorting through the contents of a box labeled "bedroom."

Rachel entered the living room and reached for the telephone mounted on the wall. "Hello," she said. "This is she . . . Oh, yes, how are you, Dr. Jeffery?" Rachel shifted her weight from one foot to the other as she listened to the doctor. "Yes, I know and I've been meaning to reschedule . . . I see," she said as she slumped against the wall and slowly slid down until she was sitting on the floor. "That would be fine," she quietly responded. "Okay, I'll see you on Monday. Thank you." Tears formed in her eyes and made their way down her cheeks as she sat quietly with the receiver still in her hand. A honking horn startled her out of her melancholy thoughts.

Rachel wiped her eyes as she walked through the front door, then outside onto the porch. She waved from the landing as the rented moving van drove up the tree-lined road and stopped in front of the house. Andrew rested his left hand on the large steering wheel and leaned forward so he could see past his passengers and returned a wave to his wife.

"Did you fit everything?" Rachel called as Thomas opened the truck door and jumped down from the passenger side. She wiped her eyes with her fingers as her brother approached.

"It's all here." Thomas walked to where Rachel was standing. "You okay?" he asked, noting his sister's puffy eyes.

"I think it's the dust," she explained and then tilted her head forward so her long blonde hair fell in front of her face.

Thomas wasn't convinced, but nodded and moved to where Andrew could see him in the truck mirrors. "Okay, come on back," he yelled.

Andrew carefully backed the yellow truck over the curb and onto the grass. The duel wheels on the rear of the truck straddled the sidewalk and left indentations in the soft turf.

When the back bumper neared Thomas, he held up his hand. Once Andrew stopped the truck, he and John got out and joined the others.

Andrew bounded up the steps and gave Rachel a peck on the cheek. "How are you two doing in there?" he asked as he patted her tummy and winked.

"Inside the house, or in here?" Rachel asked, mimicking her husband by patting her tummy.

Andrew blushed. He knew there was nothing particularly embarrassing about Rachel's quip, but still, it somehow made him uncomfortable when she talked about her body in front of others. Quite satisfied that no one else had heard Rachel's comment, he simply pointed to the house.

"You're funny," she said with a grin.

"You knew what I meant."

"Yes, I did," she admitted. "Anyway, everything Mary and I brought with us is put away. The rest should go quickly since all the boxes are labeled by room."

"Aren't you glad I suggested it?" Mary asked as she joined the others on the porch.

Rachel chuckled. "I seem to remember that being Elizabeth's suggestion."

"Oh, was it?" Mary asked in feigned innocence. She moved past her sister and met John on the steps. "I never get the credit," she complained as she wrapped her arms around her husband's broad shoulders.

John smiled at his wife. "I'm sure you would have suggested it if you'd had the chance." He slipped from Mary's embrace and pulled the large aluminum ramp from the rear of the truck and positioned it on the porch.

"All right you guys," Thomas said. "Let's get this thing unloaded." He jumped on back of the truck, undid the latch and lifted the door.

Andrew and John joined Thomas in the back of the moving van. Like an army of ants, the men latched onto boxes and pieces of furniture and moved them from the loaded truck and into the house. John and Thomas worked together on the larger items, not because of preference, but because of size advantage. John's stocky physique was still like it had been during his college football days. Thomas stood well over six feet tall, and though slim, was not short on muscle. Andrew was a little less than average height and build, but what he lacked in size, he made up for in enthusiasm. Together, the three brothers-in-law made short work of their task and soon had the entire contents of the truck moved inside the house.

Rachel and Mary worked together, emptying the last of the boxes in the bedroom and moved into the bathroom. The narrow room was the only bathroom in the house and was really too small. At the end of the room was a window that looked out toward the only other house on the street.

"Are you going to need our help again?" Mary asked her little sister as she washed her hands under the faucet that, like the rest of the house, was of 1940s vintage.

"Mom and Anna are coming over tomorrow, so I think we'll be okay. Thanks though," Rachel said as she handed Mary a towel.

"Well, okay then, but don't you overdo," Mary warned. She dried her hands, then looked into the mirror mounted above the sink and teased some of her hair with her fingers. The hint of red in the dark locks was usually only visible in the sunlight, but it showed itself regularly in Mary's temperament. "You don't want to be having this baby early."

"I won't," Rachel promised.

"How did your doctor's visit go last week?"

Rachel was silent at first, then responded reluctantly. "I didn't go."

"What do you mean you didn't go?"

"Well, we were busy getting ready to move, so I canceled the appointment," Rachel said.

Mary shook her head. "As I recall, you completely skipped the appointment two weeks before that." She turned and leaned against the vanity. "Is Andrew okay with this?"

Rachel stared at the floor, but didn't respond.

"He doesn't know, does he?" Mary asked.

"He knows I didn't go last week, but . . . ." Rachel lifted her head. "I have an appointment on Monday and I promise to keep it."

"You'd better, or Mother will have your hide. She doesn't know, does she?"

Rachel shook her head.

"Just be sure you keep that appointment," Mary said with the authority of an older sister.

Rachel nodded and looked at her watch. "You'd better get going so you can pick up your kids," she suggested.

"Yeah, I'm sure Elizabeth is ready for a break from them by now." Mary walked with her sister to the front door where the men were standing.

"You ready, Mr. Connors?" Mary asked John.

"Yes ma'am, Mrs. Connors," John replied.

Mary took John by the hand and dragged him outside. "See you guys later," she called over her shoulder.

"Bye," the others called in unison as John and Mary descended the steps and headed for their car.

"Guess I'd better be going too," Thomas said after John and Mary left.

"I sure appreciate your help, Thomas. And thanks for returning the truck for me," Andrew said.

"No problem. The store's just across the street and I told Joseph I'd be there in time to close. I guess he and Anna are going somewhere tonight."

"Well, thanks anyway," Rachel said.

Thomas shook Andrew's hand and gave Rachel a hug.

"Bye, Thomas," Rachel called after him.

Thomas turned and waved as he got into the truck, maneuvered carefully off the lawn, and drove away.

Andrew stood silently as he continued holding open the screen door.

"What are you doing?" Rachel asked.

"Just taking in the neighborhood," Andrew replied.

"Neighborhood? What neighborhood? There's one house besides ours on the whole street, and I'm not sure anyone even lives in it."

"Someone lives there," Andrew said confidently.

"How do you know?"

"There were lights on last night. Don't you remember?"

"Oh, yeah," Rachel recalled. "Anyway, why don't you come inside and relax while I fix you some dinner?

"That hardly seems fair," Andrew said. "*I* should fix dinner and let *you* rest."

"No, really, I'm fine," Rachel assured. "Just don't expect anything fancy."

"Okay, but if you're going to work, so am I," Andrew said. "I'll pick up where you and Mary left off in the bathroom."

Rachel nodded and went into the kitchen. The room was quite large, though the space was not particularly well used. All of the woodwork was pine, and painted the same white as the walls. The floor was covered with burnt orange, brown, and yellow carpet that remained from a bygone era.

"This has to be one of our first home improvement projects," Rachel called out to Andrew.

"What's does?"

"Replacing this ghastly carpet." She opened the refrigerator door and bent down to look inside. "Not too much to choose from," she said to herself. Turning around, she opened a box labeled "canned goods," and pulled out a can of chicken noodle soup.

"Soup and sandwiches be okay with you?" she hollered.

"Sounds great."

Rachel found a pot and can opener and set them on the counter next to the stove. She began rummaging through the box where she had found the pot. "Do you know where the skillet is? I can't find it with the pots and pans."

"Maybe it's in the box labeled 'dish towels,'" he suggested as he entered the kitchen.

Rachel wrinkled her forehead. "What would it be doing there?"

"I don't know. I just thought I'd suggest it," Andrew said with a wink. He stood next to his wife and helped her go through boxes.

"Here it is," Rachel announced after a few minutes of searching. "It was in with the baking trays."

"Oh yeah. I think I put it there."

"Why with the baking trays?"

"It's basically flat, isn't it?"

"I guess," Rachel said with a chuckle. "Come on, you can help me."

Andrew took the cast-iron skillet from Rachel and placed it on the stove. After opening the can of soup and pouring it into a pot, he placed it on the nearly antique appliance. "This thing has a pilot-light," he said, as he turned on the burner and adjusted the flame under the pot.

"So how do you work it?" she asked.

"Basically like the one in our old apartment. You just don't need to light it," he explained.

Rachel placed the sandwiches in the skillet and turned on the burner.

Andrew stared at the blackened pan. "Where'd you get that old skillet anyway?"

"Mom and Dad gave one to me and one to Anna when we started college."

"That's kind of a strange gift, don't you think?"

"No. We both liked to cook and Dad always insisted that things tasted better cooked on cast iron than on anything else."

"Can't say I've ever noticed, but okay."

"Well, you should notice. After all, Dad was thinking of you."

"What do you mean he was thinking of me?"

"He certainly wasn't thinking of himself, unless you're suggesting that he didn't think I was ever going to get married." She flipped the sandwiches.

"Okay, you win. The cast iron makes things taste better."

Rachel smiled smugly as she began rummaging through boxes again. She wasn't exactly sure why, but she took great pleasure in making Andrew squirm.

"Now what are you looking for?" Andrew asked.

"Bowls," she answered, "unless you want to eat the soup right out of the pot."

"It would probably taste better," he mumbled sarcastically.

"What did you say?"

"Nothing . . . ."

"Uh-huh—well for your information, smarty, it's only cast iron that adds flavor, not aluminum." Rachel moved the boxes from the top of the kitchen table and set two places while Andrew carried the pot of hot soup to the table and set it on a folded dish towel.

"Looks delicious," he said as he took his seat at the end of the table.

The couple held hands and bowed their heads as Andrew expressed thanks for their meal and the day and the blessings of their life together.

"I missed my last doctor's appointment," Rachel announced, nonchalantly, as she raised her head.

"Why?" he asked calmly.

"I figured I would have more time next week." Rachel smiled when she realized there was no need for further explanation. "But Dr. Jeffery called today and has me coming in on Monday."

Andrew nodded as he slurped hot soup from his spoon.

The two sat quietly as they ate. Rachel found herself thinking about her earlier phone call and upcoming doctor's appointment. "You seem deep in thought," she said in an attempt to avert an uncomfortable exchange.

"Just thinking about things," Andrew said.

"What things?" Rachel asked.

"About the house and the neighborhood and . . . things like that."

"There you go with the neighborhood, again," Rachel teased.

"What do you mean?"

"You can't really call two houses a neighborhood, can you?"

"I don't know why not," Andrew said. "I mean, really, how many houses does it take to make a neighborhood?"

"I don't suppose it takes a specific number . . . ."

"Exactly," Andrew interrupted. "And actually, a neighborhood is made up of neighbors, not houses."

"Okay, you got me," Rachel admitted. "So what exactly are you thinking about the neighborhood?"

"Just wondering what kind of person lives in that house at the end of our street," he said.

"How do you know it's *a* person and not people?"

"I guess I don't for sure, but I'll bet it's either an older lady or an old man," Andrew suggested.

"What makes you so sure—and why the interest anyway?" Rachel asked.

"It's kind of a quaint little old house, in its own way. It sort of reminds me of one in the neighborhood where I grew up."

"And I suppose it had an old lady or an old man living in it," Rachel said.

"Yep," Andrew confirmed. "Haven't you noticed the way that house looks?"

"I guess I really haven't paid that much attention."

Andrew continued as if he hadn't heard his wife's response. "The yard is unkempt, the vehicle has probably never been washed, and the whole house is in disrepair."

"What does all of that mean?"

"He's probably lonely," Andrew said.

"So now it's definitely a man?"

"That would be my guess. Yeah, I'm pretty sure it's a man."

"Listen to you," Rachel protested. She got up and began stacking the dishes. "What makes you so sure it's not a woman?"

Andrew stood and ran hot water into the sink. "Did you ever see an old lady driving a pickup like that one?"

"Maybe it's a couple," Rachel said.

"Nope," Andrew responded. "If he had a wife, he wouldn't have a pickup."

"Maybe it's a widow and that was her husband's truck, but she doesn't drive," she playfully suggested as she took the stacked dishes and placed them by the sink.

"Wrong again," Andrew said. He took the dirty dishes and placed them in the water. "The truck has been moved; in fact, it's been gone every time I've come down to the house this week. He must still be working some-where, but I'll bet he is widowed."

Rachel began drying the dishes Andrew had washed and placed them on the counter. "Or maybe the house is haunted and the truck comes and goes on its own," she teased.

"It's definitely strange, but I doubt it's haunted."

"I was kidding!" Rachel said. "I know it's not haunted."

Andrew washed the last spoon and drained the water from the sink. He leaned with his back against the counter and tilted his head to the side as he stared at the ceiling. "I'm just saying, there's something strange about it."

"Well, Mr. Analytical, maybe we'll just have to visit this house and meet this man, or woman . . . or both."

"Maybe I'll stop by tomorrow," Andrew suggested. "You could come with me."

"I'll have to see. Mom and Anna are coming to help tomorrow," Rachel said. "Anna's taking the day off from work, so I need to be sure her time isn't wasted."

Andrew nodded. "Yeah I've got a full day planned too. But I'll get there."

Rachel laid the dish towel on the counter and stared through the window at the last of the setting sun on the horizon. She cuddled up next to Andrew. "It's been a long day," she said. "Let's make it an early night."

Andrew took Rachel by the hand and led her to their bedroom. Just like the kitchen, the bedroom had two win-dows that met in the corner of the room. Through the windows was a clear view of the front and side yards—and the end of the street.

Andrew walked to the windows and parted the cur-tains. "There's a light . . . ." As he turned, Rachel threw a pillow that hit him in the face before he could finish his sentence.

"Let's go to bed!" she said.

chapter ✿ TWO

"Everyone has been so good to help," Rachel said. "I don't know how we could have made this move without you."

"That's what families are for," Martha said as she took off the checkered apron she was wearing and carefully folded it.

"Besides, it's been a nice break from work," Anna added.

"Are things still going well with Thomas?" Rachel asked. She pulled various clothing items from a garbage bag and sorted them into two plastic baskets in front of her.

Anna knelt across from her sister and helped sort the clothes. "Things couldn't be better," she said. "Honestly, Joseph tells me nearly everyday that he's never seen anyone with so much natural talent as a jeweler."

"It's been a blessing for Thomas to finally work at something he truly enjoys," Martha said. "And it's been good for him to work with his sister and brother-in-law." She sat in the rocking chair next to the fireplace and rested as her daughters worked together.

"So, there are no hard feelings over the money incident?" Rachel asked.

"None," Anna confirmed. "In fact, their relationship is stronger than ever."

"Trials can add a great deal of strength to a relationship," Martha added. "Too many people allow adversity to drive wedges between them. They should use those same challenges to draw them closer together."

"Spoken like a true mother," Anna said.

Martha winked at her twin daughters. "Spoken like someone who's been there."

Anna nodded. "I can't say that I welcome trials, but you're right. We choose what to make of them."

"Or what they make of us," Rachel added. She dropped a pair of blue socks in the basket of colored clothes and sat back. "It's funny, but I'm learning that the longer you're in a relationship, the more trials there are. Does that ever change, Mom?"

Martha chuckled at her daughter's question. "Our trials increase the longer we're in life, not just in relationships. Why do you ask?"

"Oh, it's just that with this move and the pregnancy and, well, everything, I find myself under a lot of stress. I worry about what that will do to our marriage," Rachel answered. "I guess I'm just scared and don't want to mess things up."

"Of course these things will add stress," Martha said, "but like we've been saying, they will provide plenty of opportunities to strengthen your marriage. And I suspect you're more anxious than scared about the pregnancy.

"Maybe," Rachel said with a sigh.

Anna finished sorting and looked at her sister. "As a newlywed, I'm certainly no authority, but Joseph and I have a much stronger relationship because of the situation with Thomas and the missing money."

"You said that—but how?" Rachel asked.

"We were both forced to explore where our priorities were and we had to decide what was really important to us," Anna explained.

"How did you do that?" Rachel asked.

"By keeping things in perspective. We simply had to realize that family is more important than money."

Martha cleared her throat and stood up. "I'd better get going if I plan to have this laundry back to you by morning, but you hang in there and let me know if there's anything I can do." She gave Rachel a hug, picked up one of the baskets from the floor and headed to the front door. "Anna, could you carry this other basket to the car for me?"

"Sure, Mom," Anna said. She picked up the basket and followed her mother. "I'll be right back," she called to Rachel over her shoulder.

Martha opened her car door and set a full laundry basket on the back seat.

"It's sweet of you to do their washing," Anna said as she placed her basket next to the other one.

"Well, I figured that would decrease the stress level a little—heaven knows she's stressed," Martha said.

"I think it would be good if I stayed with her and talked for a while," Anna said.

"I hoped you had noticed."

Anna smiled. "You should be the one staying. You're the one with all the wisdom."

Martha chuckled. "Remember a conversation we had on your twenty-first birthday?"

"About me being born first so I could help Rachel?" Anna asked.

"That's the one. I told you that someone else would come along. Then she wouldn't need you as much anymore."

"I remember," Anna said.

"Well, what I didn't tell you was that even though I knew someone else would come along to be her primary support, she would still need to rely on you at times."

"I guess this is one of those times."

Martha nodded, then gave Anna a hug and climbed into her car. "Just don't overstep your bounds," she cautioned as she closed the car door.

Anna waved as her mother drove away and then walked back to the house. She knocked on the screen door and stepped inside. "It's just me."

"I'm just putting my feet up for a few minutes," Rachel said. She was sitting in a rocking chair and rested her feet on the raised hearth in front of the brick fireplace.

"It has been a long day—mind if I join you?" Anna asked.

"Please do."

Anna slumped onto the sofa and slipped off her shoes. "Bet it feels good to have everything put away," she said.

"Almost everything," Rachel corrected. "But, yes, it does feel good. I really didn't expect to get so much done."

"Hey, this is the Cooper family."

Rachel smiled. "I guess you're right. I sure hope . . ." she paused.

"Hope what?"

16

Rachel looked down at the floor and shook her head. "Nothing," she mumbled.

"Rachel, you know we can't hide anything from each other. Now what is it?"

Rachel remained silent for a moment and then looked up at her twin sister through misty eyes. "I'm scared."

Anna sat quietly. She had sensed that something was bothering her sister but hadn't been sure what it was. Now things started to make sense. "I can only imagine," she finally said. "And you really are more scared than anxious, aren't you?"

Rachel put her face in her hands.

Anna walked to the bathroom and returned with a box of tissues for her sister. "Here, take these."

"Thank you," Rachel said as she wiped her eyes and blew her nose. "I guess I'm not cut out for this."

"Nonsense!" Anna said, resting her hand on her sister's knee. "You're a wonderful wife, and I know you'll be a wonderful mother. Now tell me what's really bothering you."

"I'm not sure that I know," Rachel said.

Anna leaned forward and looked up into Rachel's eyes. "You're worried about the baby."

Rachel nodded.

"Why are you worried? Did the doctor say something to scare you?"

"Not exactly," Rachel answered.

"What kind of answer is that?" Anna asked.

"I've skipped my past two appointments because I'm afraid . . . I'm afraid he's going to tell me there's something wrong with the baby."

"You've skipped your doctor's appointments? Rachel, if something is wrong with the baby, not knowing isn't going to help. It could even hurt."

"I know, but the last time I saw him, he drew

some blood. I've had a feeling that the results won't be normal."

"Well, maybe you can take some comfort in the fact that the doctor hasn't called. He probably would if he was concerned," Anna reasoned. She sat up and rested her back against the fireplace.

"He called me yesterday afternoon," Rachel said.

"What did he say?"

"He said he really needed to visit with me about the results of the blood tests and was anxious to get me scheduled for an ultrasound."

"How does Andrew feel about all of this," Anna asked.

Rachel looked at the floor. "He doesn't know."

"How could he not know? Doesn't he ask how your appointments have gone?"

"He knows I've missed a couple of appointments, but he doesn't know the doctor called. He doesn't know I'm scared either."

"You don't think he can tell?"

"He's a smart guy, Anna, but he's a math teacher. If there's a problem that can be analyzed and solved, no one's better at it. He's a wonderful listener. But reading emotions isn't something he's well versed in."

"Give the man some credit. He may just have a hard time explaining what he's sensing."

"That could be true," Rachel admitted. She thought back to the previous Christmas and the crisis her family had faced. Andrew had been a great support and there was no reason to doubt he would be again—especially since this potential crisis involved him directly. "I guess I haven't been fair with him and won't be until I talk about it. When I do, I'm sure he'll deal with everything better than I am."

"Give yourself some credit too," Anna said. "You're dealing with a lot."

Rachel nodded. "I'll talk to Andrew tonight. Whatever comes our way, we'll deal with it together."

"And don't forget Dad's motto," Anna said.

"I know, 'There's always tomorrow.'"

"Well," Anna said as she stood. "I think I've done enough damage around here for one day. My husband will probably want some dinner tonight, and I still need to pick up a few things from the grocery store."

"Yeah, I suppose I'd better get cooking as well," Rachel punned.

Anna smiled as she slipped her feet into her shoes. "So where is Andrew, anyway?"

"He's been spending a lot of afternoons and evenings here at the house this past couple of weeks, so he's at the school trying to catch up on a few things before the end of the year."

"Tell him hello for me," Anna said. "And let me know if I can do anything for you."

"You know I will," Rachel said.

"I'll call you on Monday after your doctor's appointment."

"Okay," Rachel said as she gave Anna a hug. She waved as her sister got into her car and drove down the street.

"Honey," Andrew said softly as he nudged Rachel's shoulder. "Honey," he repeated.

Rachel opened one eye, then the other. "What time is it?" she whispered.

"It's dinner time," he said.

"I must have dozed off," Rachel said, still trying to navigate her way through the fog of being awoken from a deep sleep.

Andrew moved the hair away from Rachel's face and kissed her. "Come on," he said. "Dinner's ready."

Andrew took Rachel by the hands and helped her to her feet. He stood behind her, interlaced his fingers with hers and rested them on her tummy, then directed her toward the kitchen. The light was out, but the soft flickering of a candle could be seen in the shadows cast through the doorway. Rachel smiled as she turned the corner and viewed the kitchen table, set for two. A single red rose in a vase made the ideal centerpiece.

"What's the occasion?" she asked.

"Oh, let me see," Andrew started. "We're in a new house, I'm caught up at work, I have a beautiful wife . . . maybe . . . ."

"Maybe . . . ?" Rachel coaxed.

"Maybe there's a new Chinese take-out on the way home from the school?"

Rachel chuckled. "I'm hoping for all of the above, but I'm betting on the last option."

"All of the above," Andrew assured. "Anyway, I thought you deserved the night off."

"I knew the kitchen looked too clean for you to have actually cooked dinner," Rachel teased. She turned and smiled at her husband. "Thank you very much."

"You're welcome," Andrew said. He directed Rachel to one end of the table, and assisted her to her seat. Then he opened the bags sitting on the counter behind her and took out several containers of hot Chinese food. "Tell me what you'd like."

"I'll try a little of everything, if that's okay."

"Comin' right up." Andrew put a colorful array of vegetables, meats, rice, egg rolls, wontons, and sauces on a plate and placed it in front of his wife. He arranged a similar medley on a plate for himself and sat at the opposite end of the table.

"This is wonderful—thank you again, honey. I really needed this tonight."

Andrew reached across the table and grasped Rachel's hand. "I know I've been a little preoccupied and perhaps even somewhat obsessive lately, but I want you to know that I'm not a total idiot."

"Andrew, I know you're not an idiot."

"Nonetheless, I want you to tell me what's bothering you."

Rachel looked a bit shocked, but just stared at Andrew.

He shook his head. "I won't accept 'nothing' or silence as an answer."

"Is it that obvious?" Rachel finally said.

"It would have to be for me to pick up on it," Andrew jested.

Rachel took in a deep breath and smiled at her husband. "You know how I told you I had missed my last doctor's appointment?" she asked.

Andrew nodded and waited for his wife to continue.

"Well, that was the second time." She waited for Andrew to say something, but he simply looked into her eyes. "I'm afraid of what he's going to tell me about the blood tests from the last time I saw him."

"Is there a particular reason?" Andrew asked.

"Just a feeling I had that something was wrong."

"Could it just be nerves?"

Rachel shook her head. "Dr. Jeffery called yesterday and said he really needs to see me so we can discuss the test results. He wants to schedule me for an ultrasound as soon as possible."

Andrew released his grasp on Rachel's hand and moved his chair around to the side of the table so he could be close to her. He kissed her on the cheek and took both of her hands in his. "Don't assume the worst," he said. "You know how doctors are. They have to consider every possibility. It could be nothing."

"Or it could be something," Rachel said. "I want to be positive; really I do, but . . . ."

"I know," Andrew interrupted. He put his arm on Rachel's neck and pulled her head to his chest.

Rachel began to cry. "What if something is wrong with the baby?"

"Everything will be fine," Andrew said. "Let's wait until we've been to the doctor on Monday before we panic."

"Then can I panic?" Rachel asked.

Andrew chuckled. "We'll see."

Rachel lifted her head and looked into Andrew's deep blue eyes. "We?"

"You don't think I'd let you go alone, do you?" he asked in surprise.

"You haven't been with me before," she said. "And really, you don't need to come."

"Yes, I do. What time is the appointment?"

"Three-thirty," Rachel said.

"Perfect. That will give me plenty of time to get here after work. Now promise me you won't worry until then."

"Right!" Rachel said. "Like I'll just forget about it."

"I'm serious," Andrew said. "Have a little faith."

"I guess you're right." Rachel sighed. "I'll tell you what; I won't say anymore about the doctor's appointment if you won't say anymore about that house at the end of the street."

"You know I was planning on stopping by that old place on my way home this evening."

"But . . . ."

"But I didn't want dinner to get cold."

"Thank you for your consideration. Now, is it a deal?"

Andrew laughed. "It's a deal. But after the doctor's appointment . . . ."

Rachel shook her head as she took two sets of bamboo chopsticks from one of the bags and handed a set to Andrew. "Let's eat before everything gets too cold."

As they enjoyed dinner together, the couple visited about nearly everything that was happening in their lives—except the doctor and the neighbor. When they concluded their meal, each took a fortune cookie from the sack.

"Perfect," Rachel said as she read the small slip of paper from inside the folded cookie. "I'm going to live long and be prosperous."

Andrew cracked his cookie and read the message.

"What does it say?"

Andrew handed the paper to Rachel.

"True happiness comes from accepting joy," she read aloud.

"What do you think that means?" Andrew asked.

Rachel shrugged and folded the small piece of paper before tucking it into her sweater pocket.

chapter ✺ THREE

Rachel tensed as the familiar smell of the doctor's office reached her nostrils.

Andrew held her hand as her grip tightened. "Try to relax," he whispered as they approached the reception desk.

"May I help you?" the young women behind the counter asked. The corners of her mouth were raised slightly.

Rachel stood silently, so Andrew finally answered. "My wife has an appointment with Dr. Jeffery."

The receptionist stared at the computer screen as her fingers rapidly navigated the keyboard in front of her. "Rachel Ingram?"

"That's right," Andrew confirmed.

"It looks like we have all your paperwork, so if you'd

like to take a seat, the nurse will come get you in just a minute."

"Thank you," Andrew said before he escorted his wife to a row of upholstered chairs against the back wall of the waiting room.

A young boy with his arm wrapped in an elastic bandage sat on the floor at his mother's feet. He used his uninjured arm to play with a wooden puzzle as his mother read a magazine.

"Rachel, we'll be fine," Andrew said.

"So you keep telling me."

Andrew put his arm around Rachel's shoulder and pulled her closer. He wanted to say more but resisted the urge, knowing that she didn't want him to say anything.

She rested her head on his shoulder and sighed. "I'm sorry I'm acting this way. It's just that I . . . " Rachel stopped mid-sentence when a nurse came into the waiting area.

"Joey, we have your x-ray," the nurse announced to the boy playing on the floor.

His mother put down her magazine and helped him pick up the puzzle pieces before following the nurse to the back.

"You were saying?" Andrew asked.

Rachel shook her head. "You know how I feel. I don't need to keep saying it."

"Go ahead and say it again if you need to."

Rachel gently laid her hand on top of Andrew's. "You're right, we'll be fine."

They sat in silent enjoyment of each other's company until Joey came running into the waiting room, sporting a colorful sling on his left arm and a lollipop in his right hand. His mother stopped at the reception desk, made a follow-up appointment and left with her son.

"Rachel," the nurse called as she stepped into the waiting room.

"That's us," Andrew said. He helped Rachel to her feet and the two of them followed the nurse down the well-lit hallway.

"Let me have you step on the scale first," the nurse said, pointing to the tall white and black device in an alcove outside the examination room.

Rachel motioned for Andrew to turn around, and then waited to get on the scale until he had done so.

"That looks good." The nurse opened the folder she was carrying and jotted down the observed measurement, without announcing what it was. She directed Rachel to a small room on the opposite side of the hall from where the scale was located.

Rachel remembered the routine from her previous visit, so she sat in the chair with oversized and unusually high arms.

The nurse took a latex strap and tied it tightly around Rachel's bicep, then used her index finger to feel the inside of Rachel's arm. After cleansing the chosen area with an alcohol soaked cotton ball, the nurse uncapped a needle and drew several tubes of blood from Rachel's arm.

Once the tubes of blood were appropriately labeled and Rachel had firm pressure on her puncture wound, the nurse directed her and Andrew into the examination room across the hall, where she preceded to hand Rachel a blue and white gown.

Rachel rolled her eyes.

"Latest designer fashion," the nurse said with a smile.

Rachel chuckled. "Thank you—I think."

"My name is Jan," the middle-aged nurse offered. Her pale pink scrubs were just the right color to cheer up anxious patients. "I'll be assisting with the examination. When you're ready, just open the door slightly and I'll be back to help get you ready for the doctor." She pulled the door tight as she left the room.

Andrew sat quietly in a folding chair while Rachel donned the gown and sat on the end of the examination table.

"You forgot to open the door," he said as he stood up and put his hand on the doorknob. "You are ready, aren't you?"

"Ready as I'll ever be."

Andrew opened the door slightly and returned to his seat. "Is the doctor nice?"

"He's very nice," she said. "I'm glad Elizabeth recommended him."

"So she's known him for a while?"

"I guess his father was her doctor when she was growing up," she answered. "Now she and James see him with their family."

Andrew nodded just as there was a knock at the door.

"Are you ready?" Jan called as she peeked around the corner of the partially opened door. She entered the room once she noted the patient clothed in the appropriate gown and seated on the examination table. "We'll get started so we can be ready for the doctor," she said as she took a fabric cuff from a drawer and placed it around Rachel's arm. "One fourteen over seventy two," she said aloud after obtaining a blood pressure reading. Placing two fingers on the inside of Rachel's wrist, she proceeded to take her pulse and respirations.

Next, Jan placed a sheet over Rachel's legs and slid the gown upward, exposing the abdomen. She pressed on Rachel's bare tummy in various locations with her hands.

"Just trying to determine the position of the baby so we can attempt to find the heartbeat with the Doppler," she explained. "This may be a bit cold," Jan announced as she squirted a blob of a jelly-like substance on Rachel's bare skin.

Rachel jumped when the cool gel came into contact with her belly.

Jan opened a cupboard and took down a small, black device that looked somewhat like an old-fashioned transistor radio with a large bulb attached by a curly cord. She placed the smooth side of the bulb in the middle of the blob on Rachel's abdomen and turned on the device. The initial static rapidly turned to a loud scraping noise, like someone brushing a piece of paper against a live microphone. Soon, the familiar sound of a heartbeat could be heard.

Rachel smiled with delight. "Is that the baby's heart?"

"That's your heartbeat," Jan answered as she continued to move the head of the Doppler until the rate of the swooshing noise increased. "There—that's the baby's."

Andrew reached up and took Rachel's hand.

Rachel turned and smiled at Andrew. Hearing the baby's heartbeat brought a welcome peace—one she hadn't felt for a long time.

Jan turned off the machine, wiped Rachel's abdomen with a towel, and then pulled the gown back down. "I'll go get the doctor," she said as she left the room.

"I told you everything would be okay," Andrew said.

Rachel squeezed her husband's hand. Her attention shifted to the door when she heard someone talking in the hallway.

"Rachel?" the gentle voice called. A tall man in his forties peeked around the corner of the partially opened door. "It's good to see you," Dr. Jeffery said as he entered the room and extended his hand toward Andrew. "And this must be Mr. Ingram?"

"I'm Andrew," he said as he stood and greeted the doctor with a handshake. There was a reassurance in the physician's firm grip and gentle nod.

"It's nice to meet you, Andrew. I'm glad you were able to come with your wife today." The doctor wheeled a stainless steel stool from the corner and sat beside his patient. "How have you been feeling, Rachel?"

"Pretty good, actually. A bit nervous, though."

Dr. Jeffery smiled as he read the notes in Rachel's chart. He assisted Rachel into a sitting position, then took a small, triangular rubber hammer from his white lab coat pocket and tested her reflexes. "Good," he muttered. "Now let's listen to your heart." Taking a stethoscope from his other pocket, he placed it on Rachel's chest. "Good," he repeated. He moved the head of the stethoscope to her back. "Take a deep breath," he instructed, several times, as he moved the device to various locations. "You've been feeling the baby move?" he asked as he returned the stethoscope to his pocket.

"Quite a bit, actually," Rachel answered.

Jan reentered the room as Dr. Jeffery was recording his findings in the chart. "Are you ready?" she asked.

"Yep," the doctor replied.

Andrew sat in silence as the doctor and nurse completed the examination on his wife. When they were finished, Jan left the room once again.

"Why don't you get dressed and then I'll have Jan bring you to my office." Dr. Jeffery suggested. "We can discuss the lab results from your last visit and answer any other questions you have."

The mere mention of the laboratory test results

seemed to almost neutralize the joy of hearing the baby's heartbeat. Andrew sensed his wife's tension, so he took the neatly folded clothes from the countertop and handed them to her.

Neither of them spoke as Rachel got dressed. Jan returned after a short time and showed them to Dr. Jeffery's private office.

The moderately large room was accented with dark-stained oak woodwork. One entire wall was made up of bookshelves, filled with a variety of literary, scientific, and medical works. The opposite wall consisted of windows, dressed with rather plain curtains, and the wall behind the desk was adorned with several framed diplomas and other types of honors.

"I wonder if he's read all of those?" Andrew asked aloud as he stared at the well stocked library. He and Rachel seated themselves in the two leather chairs positioned across from the large desk.

Dr. Jeffery came into the office and sat behind the desk. He placed Rachel's folder on the desk and opened it. He looked directly at Rachel. "I told you on the telephone that we needed to discuss the test results and get you scheduled for an ultrasound. I've taken the liberty of having Jan set that up for Wednesday afternoon. I hope that will work for you."

Rachel looked at Andrew, who nodded. "That will be fine," she said.

"An ultrasound is routine at this point in your pregnancy and up to now, we've only done routine lab work." The doctor sat up in his chair and placed his folded hands on his desk as he continued. "Once we get the results of the ultrasound, we may need to discuss the possibility of doing some more extensive testing."

Andrew expected Rachel to ask the questions he had

on his mind, but soon realized that she wasn't going to say anything. "Why?" was all he could manage to ask.

"One of the tests we did is known as a triple screen. It helps detect certain genetic disorders in the baby, and there were some results that need follow-up."

"Like what?" Andrew asked.

"Two of the three values were outside of the normal range. The alpha-fetoprotein, or AFP level, was somewhat lower than normal, and the human corionic gonadotropin, or hCG, was a little high."

"So what does that mean?" Andrew asked.

"It means we need to do further testing," Dr. Jeffery responded.

"What he means, Dr. Jeffery, is what does that tell us could be wrong with our baby?" Rachel said in a monotone voice.

The doctor took a deep breath before responding. "There is a chance that the baby could have Down syndrome—but we can't know for sure without further testing."

Rachel bit her upper lip as tears welled up in her eyes. Andrew simply stared at the doctor.

"I know this must come as a shock . . ." Dr. Jeffery paused. "Just remember, these tests are only for screening purposes. More extensive testing would be required for a definite diagnosis."

"What kind of testing?" Andrew asked.

"Well, the ultrasound is the first thing."

"And what will that tell us?" he asked.

The doctor unclasped his hands and sat up straight in his chair. "Babies with Down syndrome often have heart anomalies which can be detected by ultrasound."

"Often—but not always?" Andrew questioned. "Is there actually a way of knowing for sure?"

"The only sure way is to do an amniocentesis, which does carry some risks. But let's take first things first," Dr. Jeffery suggested.

"What difference does it make?" Rachel asked as she stared at the floor.

"What difference does what make?" the doctor asked.

"What difference does it make if the baby has Down syndrome?"

Dr. Jeffery tilted his head to one side. "I'm not sure I understand the question."

Rachel looked up at the doctor. She glared into his eyes until he became uncomfortable and shifted his questioning gaze toward Andrew. Andrew just shook his head.

"Suppose the baby does have Down syndrome—will knowing beforehand make any difference?" she questioned.

The doctor looked at the expectant mother once again. "Well . . . some parents feel that it is better that a child with that kind of disorder . . . well, that maybe it . . . ."

"Was never born?" Rachel said, anticipating what the doctor was trying so desperately not to say.

Dr. Jeffery gave a non-committal shrug. "Look, I'm just trying to prepare you for the possibilities and provide you with the information you need to make an informed decision."

"Is that the only reason to do the extended testing?" she asked.

"You do want to know, don't you?"

"I ask again," Rachel said sternly, with increasing intensity. "What difference does it make?"

Andrew reached over and took Rachel's hand. "It's all right, honey," he whispered. He looked up at Dr. Jeffery.

"I think what Rachel is trying to say, is that she's not sure she wants to go through a lot of extensive testing. Either the baby has Down syndrome or it doesn't, but either way, we're having this baby."

Rachel squeezed Andrew's hand. "That's right."

"I'm sorry if you thought I was suggesting otherwise," Dr. Jeffery said. "But knowing for sure does allow us to be more prepared at the time of delivery since Down's babies often struggle a little at first."

"Then you should be prepared just in case," Rachel suggested.

"Rachel, I know this is frightening, but I think it's too early to be jumping to conclusions of any kind. An ultrasound is routine at this point in any pregnancy, so I recommend that you go ahead with it as scheduled. Then when we get the results, you can decide how to proceed."

"I think that's reasonable. Don't you, Rachel?" Andrew asked.

Rachel sighed deeply and nodded. "I guess so," she said. Her glare softened to a gentle gaze as she looked at Dr. Jeffery. "I'm sorry. I didn't mean to be so harsh. I know you're only doing your job."

"No need for an apology," the doctor assured. He stood and walked from behind the desk.

Andrew helped Rachel to her feet. Then he shook hands with the doctor and escorted Rachel to the office door.

"Please call me if you have any questions. You'll hear from me after I get the results of the ultrasound."

"Thank you, Doctor," Andrew said.

Rachel turned around and extended her hand to Dr. Jeffery. "I shouldn't have acted that way. We need you on our side," she said.

"I am on your side, Rachel."

"Thanks," she said before exiting the office through the open door.

Andrew closed the office door behind him and followed his wife into the waiting room. He put his arm around her shoulder. "Everything will be fine," he said.

Normally Rachel would have been upset by Andrew's constant optimism, but she knew they both needed to hear it. "I know it will," she acknowledged.

"No matter what," he said.

"No matter what."

chapter ✻ FOUR

Andrew stared at the ground as he stepped from the sidewalk onto the road in front of his house. His gait was slow and deliberate. After a short distance, he stopped and squatted down. He picked up a twig that had fallen from one of the large trees lining the street. With the end of the stick, he doodled in the dirt before grasping the small branch with both hands and breaking it. As he stood up, he threw the broken pieces of wood and began walking again.

Near the end of the street, Andrew found himself standing in front of the old and mysterious house that had captivated him since his first visit to the neighborhood. It was a small brick structure with a portico stretching along the entire length of the front. The roof was covered with dried and curled asphalt shingles that were mostly devoid of the usual layer of colored gravel. The wood trim appeared as though it hadn't seen a paintbrush in decades.

Andrew stepped over the curb and made his way along the cement path to the front of the aged structure. Since the old truck was not parked at the side of the house, he wasn't sure that anyone would be home, but he had to check. Moving carefully up the steps and across the wooden deck of the porch, he found himself standing in front of the weathered door. The top half of the old oak frame supported a large oval window. He assumed the ornately etched glass was meant to be clear, though it appeared to be layered with some kind of dirt or grime. Timidly, he knocked. After several seconds, he knocked again, only more forcefully this time. For some reason, when there was no answer, Andrew grabbed the doorknob and turned it. He was grateful when the door seemed to be bolted, because he wasn't sure what he would have done if it had actually opened.

Disappointed that his attempt to meet his new neighbor was unsuccessful, Andrew stepped back and rested against the brick pillar that supported the overhang covering the porch. His thoughts drifted to an earlier time when he and a friend had attempted to enter a "haunted house" in their neighborhood. Finding the front door locked, they too, had looked through the window, but were frightened half out of their wits when they discovered the face of an old lady staring back at them. The two boys had run, screaming, from the house, only to be scolded by Andrew's father for bothering the crippled widow. He took the boys back to apologize to the woman. It was from that meeting that a wonderfully warm friendship had grown. Perhaps that was why Andrew felt drawn this old house. Maybe someone like Inga lived here.

Andrew jumped when he heard footsteps approaching from behind.

"No one is home," a voice said.

He turned to see a man standing at the end of the path where it joined the sidewalk. "So I see," Andrew said.

"He should be home around dusk," the man volunteered.

"He?" Andrew asked.

"Hank," the man said. "You know, Hank Peterman— the man who lives here. That is who you want to see isn't it?"

"I guess so," Andrew stammered. "I mean, yes."

"You don't sound very convinced," the man said. The stranger appeared to be in his late forties or early fifties. He carried some kind of long stick or pole in his hand and was wearing new jeans, a college sweatshirt, and matching ball cap. In spite of his casual dress, the man's demeanor expressed a certain air of sophistication. "Look, if you're some kind of salesman, you're wasting your time. Old Hank won't give you the time of day."

"No, I'm not a salesman," Andrew assured as he stepped off the porch and began walking down the path. "I'm the new neighbor."

"Oh, you must have moved into the Morris home."

"If you mean the house down at the end of the road, then yeah, that's right."

The man walked up the path and met Andrew halfway. He extended his right hand. "I'm William. I live over on Birch Street."

Andrew shook William's outstretched hand, but his eyes were drawn to the stick William carried in the other. "You're a ways from home, aren't you?"

William nodded. "I like to take long walks when I

get home from work and often find myself way over here. I grew up not far from here."

"So you know . . . Hank, was it?"

"I don't think anyone really knows Hank," William answered. He held up the highly polished staff in his left hand and grinned. "In case I meet any dogs."

Andrew smiled with embarrassment and nodded. "Good idea," he said when no other response came to mind.

"Well, nice meeting you, but I should be on my way so my wife doesn't get worried." William turned and started back toward the sidewalk.

Andrew had to know just one more thing before William walked away. "Hey, William, what do you know about Hank?" Andrew called.

William stopped and turned around. "Look friend, you would be wise to keep to yourself and allow Hank the same privilege."

"Why do you say that?"

"Let's just say that Hank doesn't have the best reputation."

"Why?"

William hesitated for a moment. "Not that I necessarily believe it, but some say that he murdered his wife." William shrugged and continued down the path.

A cold chill ran down Andrew's spine as he watched William reach the end of the street, turn the corner, and disappear into the distance. The very thought of living down the road from a murderer made him feel sick inside. For a brief moment he found himself considering a move to another neighborhood. "It's only a rumor," he said out loud.

Just then, the roar of an approaching engine interrupted his thoughts. The beat-up truck that Andrew had often seen parked at the side of the old house was now coming around the corner. Andrew stood back and watched as the pickup jumped over the curb, across the sidewalk, and came to rest in two ruts in the dirt. A scruffy old man stepped out of the truck and headed for the house. He swung the truck door behind him, but it failed to latch and swung back in the open position.

Not knowing what to do, Andrew called out to the old man. "Your door didn't close."

The old man either ignored Andrew or didn't hear him. Either way, he kept walking toward the house.

Andrew ran over and closed the door, then headed for the porch. "I got it for you," he said.

The old man reached the front door, turned the handle, and threw his shoulder against the heavy wood. The old door opened with a loud scraping sound. He stepped inside and pushed the door shut.

"Hmm," Andrew said. "It wasn't locked after all." He stepped onto the porch, took a deep breath, and knocked. After a silent delay, he knocked again.

"Who is it?" a gruff voice called from behind the door.

"It's your new neighbor," Andrew answered.

"What?" the voice asked through the closed door.

Andrew figured his chances of meeting the man were better if he didn't answer; that way, the man would be forced to open the door.

Slowly, the door opened. "Who are you?" the man snapped.

Andrew smiled at the aged man.

The man's wrinkled face was covered with gray whiskers that matched the uncombed hair on his head. He was dressed in a red flannel shirt underneath a pair of bib overalls.

"I'm Andrew Ingram, your new neighbor." Andrew extended his hand to the old man. "You must be Hank."

The man's deep, black, and sunken eyes glared at the intruder. He gave a quick nod and grunted. Then shut the door.

"Nice meeting you too," Andrew said aloud. Though disappointed that he hadn't managed to have a real conversation with Hank, there was a sense of satisfaction in the fact that he had met and spoken to him. During the short trek home, Andrew kept thinking about William's comment. He took comfort in the fact that William said he didn't believe the rumor about Hank.

Now that he had actually spoken to the old man, Andrew felt an even greater desire to get to know Hank. He couldn't wait to tell Rachel about their meeting and to point out that he was right. It was an old man that lived in the house, and he was . . . widowed.

The sun was going down as Andrew opened the front door to his own house. He found Rachel sitting in her rocking chair in the front room, rocking back and forth in the dark. Andrew flipped the light switch as he stepped inside. "What are you doing?" he asked.

She shaded her eyes with her hand. "Just thinking, I guess."

"Thinking about what?"

Rachel stopped rocking.

"Well?" he coaxed.

She shook her head and glared at him. "Probably the same thing you've been thinking about."

Andrew thought for a moment, and almost said something about Hank, but then realized that Rachel was most likely referring to the baby. He had been thinking about the baby when he started on his walk, but had become distracted by the old house on the corner. "Right," he said quietly. "Do you want to talk about it?"

"I'm fine," Rachel replied. "So where have you been?"

"I just went for a walk," Andrew said. "Guess who I talked to?"

Rachel shook her head. "Who?"

"The occupant of the old house. And I was right—it's an old man." Andrew sat down on the edge of the hearth and looked up at Rachel.

"That's nice," she said. "And is the house haunted?"

"Very funny," he replied. "But you may not be far off."

"Why do you say that?" she asked.

"They say that he's a murderer." Andrew sat back and rested against the brick fireplace. "What do you think of that?"

"I think it's amazing that you've been out of the house for less than half an hour and come back with neighborhood gossip."

"Who said it's gossip?" Andrew asked.

"Then you think he really is a murderer?"

Andrew wondered if he should have mentioned it at all. "Okay, it's just a rumor. But what if it's true?"

"Do you think it is?"

Andrew shrugged. "I don't know. But if it is true, I'd like to know."

"And just who told you he's a murderer?"

"His name is William. Some guy I met when I was at the house."

Rachel shook her head in confusion. "I thought you said you met the old man at the house."

"I did," Andrew confirmed.

"Then who's William?"

"He's a guy I met before the old man came home. He lives on the other side of town now, but he grew up around here. He was walking by when I was there and we started talking. He said that some people say Hank—that's the old man—killed his wife."

"And you believe this?" Rachel questioned. "They say, some people say—it's gossip, plain and simple."

"But what if it is true?"

"And what if it's not? Did you and William stop to think about this poor man's reputation? Andrew, you're spreading gossip. Admit it."

"I'm not spreading it if I don't tell anyone else," Andrew finally said in desperation to give some kind of response.

Rachel tossed her hand in the air in frustration. "I give up." She got out of the rocking chair and walked across the room toward the kitchen.

"Wait a minute," Andrew called after her.

Rachel stopped and faced her husband.

"I'm sorry, I didn't mean to upset you. I was just excited about meeting Hank."

"Did you actually meet Hank, or do you just 'feel like you know him' because of all the hearsay William shared."

"It wasn't like that. William just told me that nobody really knows Hank; that he keeps to himself."

"And that makes him a wife-killer?"

Andrew hesitated briefly before answering. "You're right," he admitted. "I guess I've gotten a little carried away. I just thought you should know what I'd heard."

"Well, you thought wrong," Rachel said. "I think

there are more important things to worry about right now."

Andrew put his arm around Rachel. "I'm sorry," he said.

Rachel shook her head. "So did you actually meet Hank?"

"Sort of."

"What does that mean?" Rachel asked.

"Well, I spoke to him. Then he slammed his door in my face."

Rachel nodded slowly. "I see. So you made a good first impression?"

Andrew chuckled. "I'm going to get to know him. You'll see."

"Right. Then he'll find out what you and William have been saying about him and he'll kill your wife," Rachel said sarcastically.

"Ha, ha," Andrew responded.

Rachel turned and continued into the kitchen with Andrew following close behind.

"Why don't you come with me next time? Maybe he won't be so rude to a woman," Andrew suggested.

"You don't think murdering a woman is rude?" Rachel asked.

"Okay, stop it. I know I shouldn't have said anything, but . . ."

Rachel leaned against the refrigerator, waiting for Andrew to continue.

"I guess I just wanted to justify my obsession with the old house." Andrew took Rachel's hands in his as he continued. "There's something about the old place. I can't explain it, but it seems to draw me in and make me want to learn all I can about it and about Hank. Does that make any sense?"

Rachel pulled her hands away from Andrew. "I'm afraid it doesn't make any sense."

"Let me explain it another way . . ."

"You don't need to explain anything," she snapped. "I understand being drawn in and wanting to learn all about something of importance that has just become a part of your life; I just thought it would be something other than that stupid old house."

Andrew moved closer and attempted to put his hand on Rachel's shoulder, but she turned and walked to the cupboard. "It's time to eat," she said, pulling out a pot and filling it with water.

chapter ❋ FIVE

"Are you nervous?" Andrew asked.

"I'm riding in a car on a bumpy road, after drinking what feels like a gallon of water, and you ask about my nerves?" Rachel responded.

"Sorry, dumb question."

"I'm just kidding," Rachel said. "I am a bit nervous. Aren't you?"

Andrew nodded. He took his right hand off the steering wheel and rested it on Rachel's knee. "Tell me again why you have to drink so much water before the test."

"I think a full bladder pushes the other organs out of the way so they can see the baby better, or something like that," she said.

Andrew nodded again.

Neither of them spoke for the few remaining miles of the drive to the hospital.

When they arrived, they held hands as they entered the large white building, navigated long hallways, and approached the reception desk at the radiology department.

"May I help you?" a young woman behind the counter asked.

"Yes, I have an appointment for an ultrasound," Rachel said. "The name is Ingram, Rachel Ingram."

"Have you been here for an ultrasound before?" the woman asked.

"No. This is my first."

The young woman smiled as she began sorting through some files. "First baby?"

Rachel nodded.

"Congratulations."

"Thank you."

The young woman smiled when she noticed Rachel's fidgeting. "There's nothing to be nervous about," she said as she handed Rachel a clipboard. "I'll need you to fill out these forms. When you're done, just bring them back to me and then I'll take you to the exam room."

"Thanks," Andrew said as he and Rachel turned and found seats in the waiting area. He picked up a magazine and began thumbing through the pages while Rachel worked on the forms.

"Are you enjoying that?" Rachel asked after several minutes.

"What?" Andrew questioned.

"That article."

Andrew looked at the title printed across the two pages of the open magazine resting on his leg. "'Diaper Rash: Has Your Baby Hit Rock Bottom?'" he read aloud with a chuckle. "Yes, as a matter of fact. I was enjoying it very much," he sarcastically replied.

"Well, can you put it down long enough to get out the insurance card?"

He took his wallet from his hip pocket, pulled out the insurance card, and gave it to Rachel.

She copied the ten-digit number from the card onto the appropriate form. "I think I'm done," she said as she handed the card back to Andrew.

The couple returned to the counter, turned in the forms, and waited a few minutes until the receptionist escorted them past the counter and into an examination room.

The young woman placed a step stool next to the padded examination table. "If you'll just lie down here, we'll get you situated."

Andrew assisted Rachel onto the table where she scooted and twisted until she was reasonably comfortable. She rested her head on the pillow and tried to relax.

The young woman placed a sheet across Rachel's legs and a towel across her abdomen. "Okay," she announced. "Tim will be right in." As she left, she drew a curtain across the room between the examination area and the door.

Andrew looked around at the room. Except for the large, technical-looking device next to the examination table, the room was quite homey. The lights were dim and a brass lamp was shining from a table situated in the opposite corner.

"You could probably sit down," Rachel suggested.

"Yeah, probably." Andrew spotted a chair and pulled it next to the bed where Rachel was lying.

She reached down and took Andrew's hand. "I love you," she said quietly.

Andrew acknowledged Rachel's comment with a nod and soft chuckle as he squeezed her hand.

The curtain in front of the door began to wave in the breeze from the hallway as a rather short, well dressed man in a mid-length lab coat entered the room. "Mrs. Ingram?"

"That's me," Rachel said, "but you can call me Rachel."

"Nice to meet you, Rachel. My name is Tim and I'll be doing the exam this afternoon." He extended his hand toward his patient.

Rachel smiled and shook Tim's hand.

"And you must be Mr. Ingram?" the technician said, looking at Andrew.

Andrew nodded. "But please don't call me Rachel," he said with a smile.

"Okay," Tim chuckled. "And what would you like me to call you?"

"Andrew would be fine."

"Very well, Andrew," Tim said as he shook Andrew's hand and then sat on the stool in front of the large machine next to the examination table.

"Rachel, did you drink plenty before coming in this afternoon?"

"Did I ever!"

"Great, then this should go fine," Tim said. "Andrew, if you'll slide your chair back just a little bit, then you should be able to get a good view of the monitor here."

Andrew complied with Tim's suggestion.

"All right, Rachel, I need to have access to your belly, so if you'll allow me, I'll get set up."

"That's fine," Rachel said.

Tim exposed Rachel's abdomen, tucking the sheet in her waistband and using the towel to cover her shirt. He took a white plastic bottle from a holder on the wall.

Tim squirted a large glob of warm gel on Rachel's belly. "I'll just use the transducer to spread this around a bit. Then we'll get started." He used the odd-looking device to smear the gel over Rachel's abdomen.

"Here we go," Tim announced as strange images began appearing on the monitor and somewhat familiar sounds emanated from the speakers.

Tim explained everything he was doing as the transducer sent images and sounds from Rachel's abdominal cavity to the ultrasound machine. Measuring some of the baby's bone lengths and organ sizes, he determined that the established due date was accurate.

Andrew and Rachel watched the screen with amazement.

"Do you want me to venture a guess at what you're having?" Tim asked at the appropriate stage of the exam.

"No!" Rachel and Andrew emphatically declared in unison.

Tim smiled. "I guess there's no disagreement between you two."

"We both like surprises," Rachel explained, her voice fading as she contemplated what she had just said. For a moment, the excitement of seeing the baby waned as she wondered if Tim could see more than the baby's gender.

Andrew squeezed Rachel's hand. He turned to Tim. "Do you see any indication of problems?"

Tim chuckled. "I'm just the technician," he said. "The tape will have to be reviewed by a radiologist for official results."

"So you can't tell us if there are problems?" Andrew asked

"I can tell you things that are within normal range

Todd F. Cope

for your dates, but beyond that, I just take the pictures."

Andrew nodded.

It was obvious that Tim was very good at what he did. His demeanor never changed, so Rachel figured there was little chance of being able to glean anything from his actions, expressions, or comments.

"Speaking of pictures, let's get some fun views and I'll shoot some stills of the baby for you," Tim suggested.

"That would be great," Rachel said.

Tim moved the transducer around Rachel's abdomen and had her change position on occasion. "You could be getting a thumb-sucker," he announced as one view clearly showed a profile of the baby.

"I wonder who that came from?" Rachel said as she giggled at Andrew's reaction. "Be sure to print that one so I can put it into the photo album next to a picture of Andrew at the age of seven."

"Hey, I got over it," Andrew defended.

Tim printed several views of the baby and handed them to Andrew. He took the towel and used it to wipe the gel from Rachel's belly. "All finished," he said as he untucked the sheet from her waistband and allowed her to pull her shirt down.

"When should we hear from the doctor?" Rachel asked as she took Andrew's hand and slid down from the examination table."

"Our radiologist will review the tape later today, so your doctor should have a copy of the report by tomorrow."

"So I guess we wait to hear from Dr. Jeffery?" Rachel asked.

Tim nodded. "Dr. Jeffery usually calls for the report the same day of the exam, so I'm sure you'll hear from him soon."

50

"Well, Tim, thank you for everything, but after drinking all that water . . . "

"First door to your right just outside," Tim said with a chuckle.

Rachel rushed passed the curtain and disappeared into the hallway.

"Thanks again, Tim," Andrew said.

"My pleasure," Tim said as he escorted Andrew into the hall. "Good luck to you both."

Andrew waved as Tim continued down the hall and disappeared around the corner. He stood deep in thought as he waited for Rachel to join him. "Well, what do you think?" he asked as she emerged from the restroom.

"I think I'm much more comfortable now."

"I'm sure you are, but what about the exam?"

"What about it?" Rachel asked, as she took hold of Andrew's hand and they headed for the exit.

"Don't you think it was obvious?"

"What was obvious?" she asked.

"That everything is fine with the baby. Didn't you notice how Tim acted when I asked if there were any problems?"

"Didn't you hear him say that he just takes the pictures?"

"I heard him, but I also watched him. I think he was telling us that everything was fine."

"Andrew . . . " Rachel started to say more, but stopped.

"What?"

"Never mind."

"No, what were you going to say?" Andrew insisted.

"Nothing."

"Rachel, you started to say something. What was it?"

Rachel sighed deeply. "Andrew, I just think you're jumping to conclusions."

"What do you mean?"

"Let's just wait to hear from Dr. Jeffery," she said as they exited the hospital and walked to their car.

"Of course we'll wait to hear from him, but I'm sure he'll just confirm what Tim has basically told us."

"Tim hasn't told us anything."

"Okay, have it your way, but I still think everything is fine."

"Andrew, I want everything to be all right with the baby just as much as you do, but I really think we should wait until we hear from the doctor before we get too excited."

Andrew was quiet as he started the car and pulled from the parking lot onto the street. "You're probably right," he finally said. "We'll just wait to hear from the doctor."

Andrew rushed to the teacher's lounge as soon as he had dismissed his last class for the day. He had called Rachel during his lunch break, but she had not heard from the doctor. He waited anxiously after picking up the telephone and dialing his home number.

"Hello."

"Rachel, did Dr. Jeffery call yet?"

"Andrew, you'll be home in half an hour."

"I know, but I didn't want to wait."

"Well, I talked to him about an hour ago," she said softly.

"And . . . ?"

"And I'm not sure we really know any more."

"What do you mean?" Andrew asked.

"He said that the ultrasound helps determine if the baby has certain traits that are common in Down syndrome."

"So what about our baby? Are there any of those traits?"

"He said that, although the baby doesn't appear to have some of the more definitive signs of Down's, it did appear that there was a slight defect– hang on a minute, I've written this down—an Atrial Septal Defect or ASD."

"So what does that mean?"

"I guess the condition is a defect between heart chambers that is frequently seen in children with Down's, but it's not uncommon in children without Down's."

"Is that a serious thing?"

"The doctor said it appears to be a small hole that may close by itself after the baby is born. If it doesn't, it can be repaired quite easily."

"Then that's good, isn't it? I mean, not that the baby has the problem, but that it doesn't mean Down syndrome.

"I guess."

"What do you mean, you guess? I think that's good news," Andrew said. "Did Dr. Jeffery weigh in on what the chances are?"

"Not really. He just pointed out that in light of the blood test and ultrasound results, there is a slightly higher than normal chance that our baby will have Down syndrome."

"Slightly higher," Andrew repeated. "If the chances are only slightly higher, I think that's good, don't you?"

"I think we don't know much more than we did before," Rachel said.

"No, I think that's good," Andrew repeated. "Sure, it would have been nice to not find A-S . . . whatever, but the fact that the real common traits weren't there . . . "

"Couldn't be seen," Rachel corrected. "The doctor did say that the traits are not always detectable by ultrasound. Further testing is the only way to find out for sure, and we've already decided not to do that, right?"

"Right," Andrew agreed. "Anyway, I don't think we have anything to worry about."

"Andrew, we need to be prepared," Rachel warned.

"I know," he replied. "So do you need me to pick up anything on the way home?"

"No, I can't think of anything. When will you be here?"

"I shouldn't be long. Love you, honey."

"I love you too."

Rachel was sitting quietly with her feet up when she heard Andrew pull into the driveway. She had been think-ing about her conversations with Dr. Jeffery and Andrew all day.

"Hey, honey," Andrew said as he came in and kissed her on the cheek. He put his briefcase down next to the fireplace and sat on the hearth. He reached over and removed Rachel's slippers and rubbed her feet.

"Oh, that feels good," she said. "What did I do to deserve this kind of treatment?"

"You made a wise choice in husbands."

Rachel laughed. "I see. And what do I need to do to ensure this kind of treatment in the future?"

"Keep the same husband I guess," Andrew teased. He leaned back against the fireplace and continued massaging his wife's feet. "You know, I've given this a lot of thought, and we probably shouldn't jump to any conclusions . . . "

"I agree," Rachel interrupted.

"We ought to do some more homework," Andrew continued. "You know, research a little—maybe talk to others."

Rachel sighed with relief. "I'm glad you feel that way. I've been worried that you were taking this whole thing a little too lightly. I know it's important to be optimistic, but you have to be realistic too. Otherwise, you could find yourself unprepared for reality."

Andrew had a look of surprise on his face as he stopped rubbing Rachel's feet and leaned forward. "Then you are worried?"

"What do mean? I've been very clear about my feelings. Of course I'm worried. Like I said, I thought you were taking things a little lightly."

"Then you agree that we should be prepared for the worst?"

"Of course I do." Rachel put her feet down and edged to the front of her chair. Putting her elbows on her knees, she leaned close to Andrew. "Do you question that?"

"It's just that a couple of nights ago, you were upset when I . . . "

"A couple of nights ago?" Rachel interrupted. She remembered the conversation she and Andrew had two evenings before and how she had cried herself to sleep. "You still don't get it, do you?"

"What do you mean? I thought . . . "

"You thought you and I have been talking about the same thing."

"Haven't we?"

"If you've been referring to our baby and the fact that it may be born with a major genetic disorder, then yes. But if you've been referring to that stupid house on the corner and the suggestion that the old man inside is a murderer, then no, we have not been talking about the same thing!" Rachel stood up and stomped into the kitchen.

"Honey," Andrew called after her. He stood and followed his wife into the kitchen. He found her staring out the window with her back to him. "Look, I'm sorry . . . "

"You keep saying that." Rachel turned and faced Andrew. "Maybe you don't understand what I'm going through because you're not carrying this baby. But I need you right now."

"And I'm here for you. Honestly, I'm here," Andrew said. He stepped forward and wrapped his arms around Rachel as she laid her head on his shoulder and sobbed.

chapter ❋ SIX

"Come on in," Anna said as she opened the front door and invited her twin sister inside.

Rachel warily entered Anna's front room. "What are you up to?" she asked. It wasn't uncommon for Anna to invite her sister to come for a visit, but Rachel had been suspicious since the invitation was for a specific day and time.

"Why would I be up to anything?" Anna asked.

Rachel breathed a sigh of relief when it was obvious that her sister's front room was unoccupied. "I was afraid that you had organized a surprise baby shower or something."

"Does that really seem like something I would do?"

"Let me think," Rachel began. "There was the surprise bridal shower and the surprise engagement party.

Let's not forget the surprise, and may I add embarrassing, no-date-to-the-prom sympathy party in high school. Should I go on?"

"Excuse me, but it was a Prom Protest Party and in all fairness, I could only host it because I didn't have a date either," Anna said. "Besides, every girl there was in the same boat, so I don't know why you found it so embarrassing."

"Probably because you placed an ad in the school paper announcing the party and inviting any girl without a date to attend."

"Oh yeah."

"It was bad enough not having a date, but then you had to advertise the fact to everyone."

"My name was the one at the bottom of the ad, not yours."

Rachel chuckled. "I suppose you forgot about the opening line that started, 'My sister and I . . . ?'"

Anna laughed. "I guess that was kind of unfair."

"Well, never mind. I forgave you back then. Besides, I was simply making the point that you do have a history of trying to surprise me," Rachel said.

"And you really don't like it when I do?" Anna asked.

"I have to admit that the parties are always fun, but I really don't like being the center of attention."

"Then you're okay with the occasional surprise party?"

Rachel laughed. "Does it really matter?"

Anna thought for a moment. "If you really didn't want me to keep surprising you, you know I'd stop."

"I know you would," Rachel said.

Anna smiled at her sister. "Come on, let's get something to eat," she said, walking toward the kitchen.

Rachel followed her sister around the corner and into the kitchen just in time to hear, "Surprise!"

"I just couldn't resist," Anna said sheepishly as Rachel entered the room.

Rachel shook her head and smiled as she looked at the room full of women. "Thank you all for coming," she said in a voice too soft for most of them to hear.

As she looked around the room, Rachel was grateful that Anna had only invited family and a couple of close friends. Besides their mother, sister, and sister-in-law, there were James and Elizabeth's daughters, Lisa and Jessica, Andrew's sister Brenda, and Martha's friend Sarah. Rhonda, Anna and Rachel's best friend from high school, was also in attendance.

"Why don't we all move onto the patio," Anna directed as she made her way through the small crowd and opened the French doors leading outside.

"Thank you, Anna," Rachel said as she followed the others past her sister through the open door.

"Are you sure you don't mind?" Anna asked.

Rachel nodded. "I'm sure. I still don't like being the center of attention, but this is probably just what I need right now."

"I'm glad," Anna said. "Now go out and mingle for a while."

After plenty of party conversation, the women gathered for a few baby-focused party games and then watched as Rachel opened the gifts.

Martha, Mary, Elizabeth and Anna had joined together in purchasing an old-fashioned bassinet, and Lisa and Jessica proudly presented Rachel with a collection of baby toys. Brenda gave her a stroller that she had purchased with her mother's financial help, and Sarah gave her a beautiful blue and pink baby quilt. Rhonda gave her a couple of outfits suitable for either a little boy or girl.

"Everything is lovely," Rachel said. "I really didn't expect anything like this."

Anna and Martha slipped from the gathering and returned to the kitchen to prepare the food.

After they left, Rhonda asked to be excused so that she could meet her fiancé at the airport. "You know I love a good party, but I'm afraid Steve wouldn't understand," Rhonda teased.

"I suppose you're right," Rachel agreed. She went with Rhonda to the kitchen so Rhonda could say good-bye to Anna and then walked with her to the front door. "You'll have to bring Steve over. It's been a while since we've seen him."

"I will," Rhonda promised, and gave Rachel a hug.

As Rhonda drove away, Rachel thought about the so-called "Prom Protest Party" and smiled. Rhonda had left that party early as well, only that time she was going to spy on Steve and his prom date.

Rachel returned to the kitchen and helped Martha and Anna with the final food preparations.

Following the light meal and some additional socializing, Sarah began to squirm. "I'd better leave so I can make it home before it gets too late," she announced.

Rachel smiled at Martha, who looked at her watch and shook her head. It was only 4:00 p.m. and Sarah lived less than 15 minutes away.

Rachel and Anna accompanied Sarah to the front door and Rachel thanked Sarah for coming and for the lovely quilt. "It will go perfectly in the bassinet," she said.

"I'm glad you like it, dear," Sarah said as she stepped through the door and onto the front porch. "Now, don't you do too much lifting. You can settle into your new house after the baby is born." Sarah continued speaking as she made her way carefully down the steps and onto the sidewalk. "It can harm the baby if you lift too much, you know. I know a woman who lifted a lot while she was expecting and her baby was born with a spindly neck. Dreadful looking child," she mumbled.

The twins found it difficult to keep from laughing out loud, but managed to restrain themselves.

"I promise to be careful, Sarah," Rachel managed to say. "Thanks again for coming."

Sarah waved as she walked across the street, climbed behind the wheel of her thirty-year-old yellow Cadillac and honked the horn as she pulled away.

"I guess I won't be lifting much," Rachel teased.

"Just remember," Anna cautioned, "Sarah's advice may have saved Mother's life last Christmas."

Rachel chuckled. "You're right, but somehow I don't think this falls into the same category. I will, however, give it appropriate consideration."

"That sounds fair to me," Anna said as she began to laugh.

"What's so funny?" Martha asked as the twins entered the kitchen where the others were clearing the food and doing dishes.

"They were with Sarah," Mary said.

Martha nodded in understanding. "She means well."

"I know," Rachel said.

"Was her advice good?" Elizabeth asked.

"Let's just say I won't be doing a lot of lifting for the next several months."

"Why, would that give the baby an extra ear or something?" Mary sarcastically asked.

"No, a spindly neck," Rachel corrected.

Everyone in the room began to laugh.

"Sounds like this Sarah is quite a character," Brenda said.

"She's a very nice woman and a lovely friend," Martha responded as she dried the last glass and placed it in the cupboard. "Sometimes her ideas may seem a little strange, but we all have funny ideas at times."

"I suppose you're right," Brenda said. She drained the dishwater and dried her hands on a towel hanging over the handle of the oven. "So, Mrs. Cooper, you've had several children—is there anything to some of these old wives' tales?"

"I'm certainly no expert, but I think most of them are just that: old wives' tales."

"But I've heard that if you do certain things during the early stages of pregnancy, you can cause developmental problems," Rachel said.

"I suppose that's true. But you know, women have been carrying and delivering babies for a long time, and most of them are free of any major problems," Martha said as she sat down in a chair beside the kitchen table.

Rachel pulled a chair from under the table and sat down next to her mother. "Still, it does seem that a lot of babies are born with problems these days," she said.

"You're not worried, are you Rachel?" Brenda asked.

Rachel and Andrew hadn't said anything to his side of the family about the early test results, so she wasn't sure how to answer.

"Every expectant mother worries," Elizabeth said. "It's part of the job description."

Brenda laughed. "I'm sure you're right." She walked over to Rachel and gently rubbed her shoulder with her open hand. "I need to be going."

"Thanks for coming," Rachel said. "I wish your mother could have been here."

"Yeah, she would have liked to have been here, but you know how it is."

"I understand," Rachel said. "I wouldn't drive six hours for a baby shower either."

"Anyway," Brenda continued, "she sends her love."

Rachel stood and gave her sister-in-law a hug. "We'll have you over for dinner sometime."

Brenda nodded. "Anna, thanks for inviting me. It was good to see all of you again."

"We're glad you could come," Anna said.

"I'll see myself out," Brenda said as she headed toward the front door.

"Bye," everyone said in unison.

Rachel sat down again. "Thanks for helping me out, Elizabeth. I wasn't sure what to say."

"You're welcome."

"I assume Brenda doesn't know," Anna said.

Rachel shook her head. "I've had no problem being very open with all of you about it, but I feel that Andrew should be the one to tell his family."

"So why hasn't he?" Mary asked.

"I guess he doesn't think there's anything to tell them," Rachel answered.

"You mean he's in denial?" Mary said. She looked at the others who remained in uncomfortable silence. "That didn't come out right. I meant, he doesn't believe there's sufficient cause to alarm them."

"Nice recovery," Martha jabbed. "But I'm sure you're right, Mary."

"I'm sure it's difficult for both of you, Rachel, but everything will turn out fine," Elizabeth said.

Rachel nodded.

"Well, Mary, we need to be going," Elizabeth said. "Lisa has homework to finish before we go to the movies tonight."

"Guess I'd better come, then, if I want a ride home."

"I can take you if you want to stay a little longer," Martha offered.

"No, that's out of your way," Mary said. "Besides, my mouth's only big enough for one foot."

The others chuckled at Mary's remark. They were all used to her straight-forward manner and had come to accept or ignore her occasional poorly worded comments.

"I'll go get the girls then," Elizabeth said as she went back to the patio.

"So what are John and the boys doing?" Rachel asked Mary.

"I left them cleaning the garage," Mary said. "I told them there would be no camping trip this summer unless my car would fit in the garage by the time school finished for the year."

"You haven't left them much time, since school gets out next week," Martha said.

Mary shrugged her shoulders.

Elizabeth came inside with her two daughters. "Give Grandma a kiss," she instructed the girls.

Lisa and Jessica each kissed Martha on the cheek.

"You girls be good," Martha told them.

"We will," they said in unison.

"Now hug Aunt Rachel and Aunt Anna, and tell them thanks for inviting you," Elizabeth said.

Once again, the girls obeyed their mother.

"We'll see you all later," Elizabeth said as she and her girls headed for the front door. "We know our way out."

"Good-bye," Mary said as she followed behind her sister-in-law and nieces.

"Bye," Martha, Anna, and Rachel called after them.

Anna pulled up a chair and sat at the kitchen table across from Rachel and Martha. She gazed at her twin before speaking. "Want to talk about it?"

"I'm fine," Rachel replied.

"That didn't answer my question," Anna said with a smile.

Rachel sighed. "Then . . . " She paused. "Yes and no, I suppose."

Martha smiled at Rachel's response to her sister's query. "Elizabeth was right," she said. "All mothers worry. There's nothing wrong with that."

Rachel's nod indicated that she agreed with her mother, but the expression on her face said otherwise.

"I think you're more worried than you're letting on," Anna said.

"Or perhaps more than you're aware," Martha suggested. "How can we help you?"

"I don't know," Rachel answered. "I'm not even sure I understand my feelings right now."

"Not that I'm trying to dismiss your feelings, but that is natural during pregnancy too," Martha said. "Your emotions tend to be out of sync much of the time."

Rachel nodded and wiped her eyes. "That I can accept," she said. "I never know whether to laugh or cry, and sometimes I want to do both at the same time."

"Is that how you feel right now?" Anna asked.

"I guess it is," Rachel admitted.

"So what's bothering you most?" Martha asked.

Rachel looked at her mother and then at Anna. "Andrew just doesn't understand," Rachel sobbed. "Sometimes he doesn't seem to care."

Anna moved her chair next to Rachel's and put her arm around her sister's shoulder. "It's okay. He probably doesn't understand, but I'm sure he cares."

"Then why doesn't he act like it? All he wants to talk about is the stupid old house on our street"

"You know you can always talk to me," Anna said. "You know I'm always here for you."

"I'm confident that Andrew is too, Anna," Martha said. "That's more important right now. Remember, there are boundaries."

Anna recognized Martha's gentle rebuke. She knew she had to be careful to support her sister without undermining Rachel's relationship with Andrew.

"We have to remember that men and women deal with stress differently," Martha continued. "Andrew's probably just dealing with things in his own way."

"But Mom, he doesn't seem to care about my feelings," Rachel protested.

"And what about *his* feelings?" Martha asked. "Have you ever stopped to consider what he may be going through?"

Rachel blew her nose into a tissue and shook her head. "I guess I haven't," she quietly admitted.

Martha leaned forward and placed her hand on Rachel's knee. "Perhaps you should."

"But how am I supposed to understand his feelings when I can't even understand my own?"

"That's something you and Andrew will have to work out together," Martha said.

"Can't we have any help?" Rachel asked.

Martha chuckled. "I'll help, but I won't interfere." She looked at Anna, who sat silently. "How about you, Anna? Can you help without interfering?"

Anna smiled. "I'll do my best," she said.

"That's not good enough," Martha returned with a wink.

"Okay I'll help, but I won't interfere," Anna promised.

"Good," Rachel said. "Then you can help me figure out how it is that I can love Andrew, yet be so angry at him right now."

"What are you angry about?" Anna asked.

"I told you. All he seems to care about is that stupid old house and that stu . . . and the man that lives there. Sometimes we'll be talking about the baby, or so I think, and come to find out, he's been talking about our neighbor the whole time. It's like Andrew's more interested in him than the baby."

"Okay, Rachel," Martha said. "Think about Andrew and what he's feeling. He's a pretty quiet guy, isn't he?"

"Yeah."

"And he tends to be analytical—always figuring things out logically and solving problems, right?"

"Well, he is a math teacher," Rachel said.

"So, besides the fact that he's generally quiet anyway, isn't it possible that Andrew doesn't want to talk about the baby because he can't use logic to explain his feelings?"

"So you're saying that maybe the house and Hank are just things he can think about—a problem he can solve?"

"We may be oversimplifying, but yes, I think that's very possible," Martha said. "You and Andrew will often see things differently and react to them differently, but that doesn't necessarily mean either of you is wrong."

"Mom's right," Anna said. "It's just like when Joseph and I were dealing with the lost money. He wanted to figure it out logically and I wanted to believe the answer was in my dreams. And in the end, it took both."

"This is something you and Andrew will have to work on together," Martha said. "Just be patient, and he'll come around to recognizing your needs—just like you'll eventually recognize his."

"Okay, then, who's going to help him?" Rachel asked.

"What do you mean?" Martha questioned.

"Well, I have my family to help me keep things in perspective, but he's not that close to anyone," Rachel said.

"Someone will be there," Martha said confidently.

"Like who?" Rachel asked.

Martha shook her head. "I don't know for sure, but someone."

Rachel sighed heavily and nodded.

"Do you feel any better?" Martha asked.

Rachel shrugged and nodded again.

"Rachel, there's something else, isn't there?" Anna asked softly.

"Not really," Rachel said as she stared at the floor. "We've pretty much covered it."

Anna reached over and lifted Rachel's chin. She peered into her sister's eyes. "You know you can't hide anything from me," she said.

Rachel didn't speak, but her eyes began filling with tears again.

"What is it?" Anna asked.

"I just don't know if I can live with . . . " Rachel began to say, but her voice faded into quiet weeping as she buried her face in her hands.

"Can't live with what?" Martha asked.

"What if I've done something to harm my baby?" Rachel sobbed.

Anna lifted Rachel's head and looked her in the eyes. "You haven't harmed your baby," she whispered, then embraced her sister and cried with her.

chapter ❀ SEVEN

Andrew sprinted up the steps to the old library. It was a plain looking brick building that sat across from City Hall. Its simple architecture was quite a contrast to the ornate structure on the other side of Main Street.

He approached the desk and waited for someone to assist him.

An older woman was perched on a stool behind the counter. She was speaking on the telephone and motioned that she would only be a moment.

Andrew rested his back on the counter and surveyed his surroundings while waiting. Though he and Rachel had lived in town for several years, he had never had occasion to go the public library. The school library at work had always met his needs up to this point. But now he needed to do some real research.

It surprised Andrew that things were so quiet on a Saturday afternoon. It appeared that he was the only other person in the library besides the librarian. He leaned forward a little to peer between the rows of books near the front, but he seemed to be the sole patron. With no one else requiring her assistance, perhaps he could have the undivided attention of the librarian.

"How can I help you?" the woman asked after hanging up the telephone. Her inviting smile made Andrew smile in return. She was wearing a plain white blouse and black skirt. Her gray hair was put up in a bun, and in almost every respect, she reminded Andrew of Mrs. McKenzie, one of his childhood Sunday school teachers.

"Yes, Mrs. . . . ?" he started.

"Huntington," she volunteered.

"Mrs. Huntington," Andrew repeated. "I'm looking for a newspaper article from several years ago."

"How many years?" Mrs. Huntington asked.

"Well, I'm not exactly sure," Andrew said.

Mrs. Huntington folded her arms across her chest and smiled. "What's the article titled?"

"Actually, I don't know."

"Which paper?" she asked.

Andrew shrugged his shoulders. "You see, I'm not even sure there is an article. I just think there is."

Mrs. Huntington lowered her head and glared over the top of her glasses, but didn't say anything.

Looking into her squinted eyes, Andrew could tell what she was thinking. "I know it sounds strange, but I'm trying to find out if something I heard about actually happened. That's why I don't know exactly what I'm looking for."

"Sounds like you have a problem," she said with a straight-lipped smile.

"Yeah, kind of," he admitted. "Do you think you can help me?"

She shook her head, almost as if in disgust. "I'll see what I can do," she said sternly, but then her lips curled and she began to chuckle. "Come over here with me," she instructed as she left her position behind the counter and walked around the corner. She led Andrew past the drinking fountain and a couple of lounge chairs to the back wall of the library and stopped in front of what looked like several dozen wooden racks.

The racks were lined up against the wall, each one supporting six wooden dowels. Each dowel had several open newspapers draped over it. "Here is every edition of the local paper for the past fifty years," she said. "That's the only newspaper we keep."

"I was expecting you to show me to a microfiche reader," Andrew said.

Mrs. Huntington shook her head. "This is a small library in a small town."

Andrew quickly did the math in his head and realized that if Mrs. Huntington was speaking the truth, he was looking at 2600 copies of the weekly paper. He used his index finger to point at the racks and began counting.

"There are fifty of them," the librarian said. "A full year on each rack."

Again, he calculated the numbers in his head. "So there's two months worth of papers on each dowel?" he asked.

"That's right."

"Wow," was all Andrew could manage to say.

"If we had more room, we'd keep more," she said

"That's incredible," he said as he stared at the local

history in print. "How often do people refer to these?"

"Not too often but often enough," she answered. "So tell me about this article that may or may not exist and when the event it's reporting may or may not have happened."

Andrew chuckled. "I guess I'm not being very helpful, am I?"

Mrs. Huntington shook her head.

"I'm going to guess that it was close to fifty years ago," Andrew said.

"Okay, now we're getting somewhere. Come down here," Mrs. Huntington instructed. She continued talking as they walked. "Unfortunately, the newspapers are not catalogued, so you'll have to go through each one individually."

Andrew followed as Mrs. Huntington took him to the racks at the end of the row. He noticed that the papers hanging on the dowels were yellowing and somewhat tattered the further they went.

"Here we are," she said as they reached the end of the row.

The lighting in this part of the library was somewhat dim and it took Andrew's eyes several seconds to adjust. As his vision cleared, he approached the last rack and touched the paper. He wasn't sure what he expected, but it felt like any other old paper. Still, he felt like he needed to show reverence for this small town's history which was right before his eyes. He knew that if the reporting of fifty years ago was anything like the current reporting in the paper, much of the information was likely to be very personal.

"Be very careful," Mrs. Huntington said. "Paper that old becomes very brittle."

Andrew nodded. "So, can I just lift off a paper and look at it?"

"Decide which stack you want to start with and I'll help you lift it off and carry it to that table," she said as she pointed to a long wooden table in the corner behind them.

"I guess we'll start with the first one," he said.

"Very well," Mrs. Huntington said as she took one end of the chosen dowel and motioned for Andrew to take hold of the other end.

Carefully, they lifted the dowel up high enough for the hanging papers to clear the rack and carried them to the corner. They placed them on the table, and Mrs. Huntington lifted the top fold and opened the papers so that they lay flat. She took the dowel they had been draped over and put it back in place on the rack.

"There you go, Mr. . . . " she began. "You'll have to excuse me, but I don't think I even asked your name."

"Andrew," he said.

"There you go Mr. Andrew, papers from fifty years ago," she said with a smile.

"Actually, Andrew is my first name."

Mrs. Huntington blushed. "Oh, I'm sorry, Andrew. Then I guess you'd better call me Edith."

"Okay, Edith," he said as he carefully ran his open hand over the paper.

Just then, the sound of a brass bell could be heard from the front of the library.

"Someone's just come in," Edith said. "I'll have to leave you to it for now, but be sure and call me when you're ready to put these back."

"I will," Andrew said as he began lifting the corners of the pages.

Edith walked back along the row of newspaper racks and disappeared around the corner.

Starting at the top, Andrew leafed through three

pages before he came to the front page of the next edition. He carefully lifted the first edition off the stack and placed it on the opposite end of the same table. "Jenkins wedding well attended," he read aloud from the front page. He smiled as he looked at the photo of the handsome newlyweds in the center of the article.

Andrew read all of the headlines on the front page of the paper, opened it up and began reading headlines from page two. PIG DISPUTE DECISION PENDING; NEW BANDSTAND NEARLY COMPLETE; MAYOR WELCOMES DIGNITARIES; SCHOOL YEAR ENDED. He couldn't help but chuckle as he perused some of the stories that made news during that time.

Andrew looked at each page of all twelve editions of the newspaper, but found nothing that brought him any closer to the truth. He returned to the rack where the papers had come from and retrieved the dowel. Placing it in the center of the opened newspapers, he carefully folded one half of the stack over the dowel.

As instructed, Andrew headed toward the front of the library to find Edith and request her assistance. As he rounded the corner, he heard the familiar ring of the brass bell hanging over the front door and wondered if new patrons were entering or if Edith would now be available. He found her behind the front counter, placing an index card in a file drawer.

"Are you ready for more?" she asked as she looked up and saw Andrew gazing in her direction.

"I am, if you have the time."

She looked around at the empty room. "Looks like everyone is doing fine."

"Is it always this quiet?" Andrew asked. "I mean, I really thought it would be busier than this."

"Usually it is, but it's the weekend before school gets

out. The kids don't have any homework, and the sunshine sure is inviting. Only a fool would be at the library," she said with a smile.

"Thanks," Andrew said with a laugh.

"Just remember, I'm here too," Edith said. "Come on, let's put those papers back."

Once again, Andrew followed Edith to the back of the library. Together, they returned the newspapers to their appropriate resting place on the rack.

"Did you find what you were looking for?" she asked.

"No, I'm afraid I didn't," Andrew said.

"At the risk of adding to my confusion, may I ask again exactly what you're looking for?"

Andrew found Edith's mild sarcasm refreshing. He appreciated anyone with a good sense of humor, but particularly someone who was expected to be somber.

"I'm looking for anything about the death of a woman," he said.

"Any particular woman, or will the first one you find suffice?" she teased.

Andrew shook his head and smiled. "A woman by the name of Peterman, I believe."

Edith's jovial expression suddenly became solemn. "Did you say Peterman?"

"That's right."

"What was her first name?" Edith asked.

"I don't know," Andrew answered. "Why? Did you know her?"

Edith leaned against the table. Then, folding her arms across her chest, she stared at the newspaper racks. "Andrew, what is it you want to know about Mrs. Peterman's death."

"I want to know the cause."

"What interest do you have in the cause of her death?" she asked.

"I'm just curious, that's all."

"People aren't 'just curious' about something like that unless they have a reason to be," Edith suggested. "What are you? Some kind of writer or something?"

"No, I'm not a writer. I'm a math teacher," Andrew said. "It's just that . . . look, let me level with you. My wife and I just bought a house down the street from Hank Peterman. Ever since we moved in, I've had a feeling there was something strange about Hank and his old house. The other day I stopped by to introduce myself to him and bumped into a guy who told me that Hank is rumored to have killed his wife. I just wanted to know if it was true. That's why I'm interested."

"What did the man tell you about Hank?" Edith asked.

"Only that some people say he murdered his wife. He said he wasn't sure if he believed them."

"But it sounds like you do?"

Andrew felt a little sheepish. "You sound just like my wife," he mumbled.

"Then she must be a pretty wise woman," Edith said with a wink.

Andrew nodded. "You make it sound as though I'm out to get Hank or something."

"Are you?" Edith asked.

"No! That's not it," Andrew defensively returned.

"Then what is it?"

Normally, Andrew would have been annoyed by this type of interrogation, but somehow it seemed okay coming from Edith. "It's hard to explain," he said.

"Try me."

Andrew smiled. "I was interested in Hank before I

heard anything about the rumor. Maybe it's his house. It kind of reminds me of an old house in the neighborhood where I grew up. I guess I hoped that Hank would be like the old lady who lived in it."

"Maybe he is," Edith suggested.

"I hope he is, even if the rumors are true."

Edith nodded, but didn't look convinced. "Did you meet Hank the other day?"

"I introduced myself to him when he got home that evening, but I'm not sure that counts."

Edith tipped her head forward and looked at Andrew over her glasses.

"Well, when I told him who I was, he nodded and grunted before he slammed the door in my face."

Edith chuckled. "Well, I've never met the man myself, but from what others tell me, you've had as much of a conversation with him as anyone else. I think he likes you."

"Right," he said.

"You're probably the first person in a long time to have any interest in him. He probably appreciates that."

"He didn't act like he appreciates it much," Andrew said.

"I'll bet he does—or at least he will if you really are interested in who he is more than in what he might have done," Edith said. "If that's the case, I'll help you find out about the rumors. I have to admit, I'm a little curious myself."

"Have you heard any of the rumors?" Andrew asked.

Edith remained silent for quite some time; then she turned and looked at Andrew. "I don't believe I've heard anything of them for more than . . . a lot of years," she said.

"What have you heard?" Andrew asked.

"Oh, you know teenagers. They love a scary story. Back then, none were scarier than the ones about the Petermans," she said.

Andrew got a familiar sick feeling in his stomach. Though he had come to the library seeking information about the Petermans, now he wasn't sure he wanted to hear it. "Stories about murder?" he finally asked.

Edith nodded.

"What did you hear?" Andrew asked.

"All kinds of things about how he went mad one night and killed his wife and baby."

"Baby?" Andrew asked.

Edith sighed heavily. "Remember that these were just stories told by teenagers. Nothing was ever proven."

"What about the baby?"

"I don't know," Edith said. "I guess the baby was just part of the story. But you know how things change the more they're repeated. Things become more frightening and gruesome every time they're retold."

Andrew stared into the distance.

"What is it Andrew?"

"I didn't know there was a baby," he said.

"Have you been listening to me?" Edith asked. "The baby may have been a fabrication to enhance the story."

"But what if it wasn't?" Andrew asked.

"That's part of the reason I want to help you find out what really happened. If Hank Peterman is innocent, then everyone should know the truth. If he's guilty, then he's probably in pain—after fifty years, he's due for some relief."

Andrew nodded but remained silent.

Edith reached over and put her hand on Andrew's shoulder. He looked up at her and she smiled softly.

"Are you and your wife expecting a baby?" she asked.

Andrew nodded again. "How did you know?"

"Just a hunch," Edith said. "Anyway, let's see what we can find out about the Petermans."

"So far, I haven't been able to find anything," Andrew said.

"Let me think about this," Edith said. "When we were scaring each other as teenagers, the murders had supposedly happened nine or ten years earlier. That would mean I was probably about . . . never mind how old I was, but these newspapers don't go back far enough."

"Why not?" he asked.

"We keep the most recent issues of the paper behind the front desk," she explained. "When we have a full year, they are placed on the last rack, after the oldest issues are removed. Then we move the rack with the most current year from the back of the row to the front."

"And what do you do with the old issues?" Andrew asked.

"I'm sad to say that we're instructed to destroy them. As you can see, we don't have a lot of room for storage," Edith said, pointing around the room.

"So now what?" he asked.

"I said we're instructed to destroy them. I didn't say we *do* destroy them," she said with a wink.

Andrew grinned. "Do you mean to tell me that you still have those back issues somewhere?"

"Follow me," she said as she moved away from the table and walked to a door labeled "Employees Only." She opened the door to reveal a dark stairway. After Edith flipped on the light, Andrew followed her up into an attic room. The musty air felt thick and heavy. There were dozens of dust covered boxes stacked on the floor around the room. The thick coating of dust on the floor was disturbed by footprints that lead to and from the top of the stairs and two large tables directly under the single light bulb hanging in the center of the room.

The tables were similar to the ones downstairs where Andrew had been reviewing the old newspapers, only much larger. On the far end of one of the tables was a large stack of open newspapers. The only thing on the other table was an old manual typewriter.

Edith directed Andrew to the open papers. "Here you are," she said. "Another ten years of history."

"How long have you been putting the old papers up here?" Andrew asked.

"Ten years, of course," Edith answered.

"This is great," Andrew said as he peeled back the corner of the papers. "Where do you think we should start?"

Edith walked over to the stack and looked at small slips of paper protruding from the edges. "These strips divide the papers by month and year." She flipped through some papers and finally stopped when she found the issue she'd been looking for. "Right here," she said. "Help me lay these other papers aside."

After blowing the dust from the top paper, Andrew assisted Edith in laying the pages face down next to the stack until the front page of the newspaper she had selected was revealed.

"You can start right here," she said. "I really need to go back down and watch the front, but you can take all the time you need—at least until closing time."

"Any idea what I should be looking for?" Andrew asked.

"You're the math teacher," she said with a chuckle. "I don't know. Look for the name Peterman, I guess."

"Right," he said. "I'll come get you if I find any-thing."

Andrew watched as Edith made her way down the stairs and closed the door behind her. He soon lost himself in the work of reading headlines. Like the papers downstairs, the stories and articles varied in subject from page to page and from paper to paper. Unlike the papers he was used to reading, these papers were not divided into specific sections. Similar stories were not always grouped together. He found it particularly amusing when wedding announcements were placed right next to obituaries, or when an ad promoting the services of the town's doctor was located directly above an advertisement for the local undertaker.

After about an hour, Andrew had not come across anything about the Petermans. The dim light of the attic room was making his eyes ache, so he decided to call it quits for the day. Leaving the papers as they were, he made his way down the stairs. The bright light forced him to shade his eyes when he first opened the door, and he headed for the front of the library.

"Did you find something?" Edith asked as he rounded the corner at the front desk.

Andrew shook his head. "No. That isn't the best light for reading up there."

"No it isn't," Edith agreed. "I'll bring a desk lamp from home on Monday."

"There's no rush," Andrew said, "I probably can't come back until next Saturday."

"I'll be here Monday," Edith said.

"Won't you need to stay down here?" Andrew asked.

"Of course I will when the library is open, but there's nothing stopping me from coming in early or staying late, is there?"

"What about Mr. Huntington?"

"Mr. Huntington will be just fine where he is. In fact, he's better off than we are," she said as she lifted her eyes heavenward.

"Oh, I'm sorry," Andrew said. "I guess I shouldn't have assumed."

"Don't worry. I've been without him for a long time," she said. "He died just a year and a half after our marriage, before we were able to have any children. I guess some might call it a lonely life, but it's all I've known for so many years that I don't really give it much thought."

"You know something Edith? You are a remarkable woman," Andrew said.

"You have a problem with snap judgments about people, don't you?"

Andrew shook his head and laughed. "Maybe sometimes, but not today."

Edith smiled. "You should probably be getting home to your wife. She's probably worried sick about you and she'd be particularly upset if she knew you were spending your time with another woman."

Andrew smiled as he nodded and walked out the door.

chapter EIGHT

Andrew rolled over and hit the snooze button a second time in order to stop the incessant noise coming from his alarm. The radio station wasn't quite tuned-in, so there was more static than music, and for the moment, the simple push of a button seemed less complicated than a dial adjustment.

Rachel was sitting up in bed reading. "Are you ever getting out of bed?" she asked.

"Ummm," Andrew groaned.

"Come on, sleepyhead. The day's not getting any longer."

"I'm working on it," he mumbled.

Getting up in the mornings wasn't usually a problem for Andrew, but he had put in a long day at work the day before. School had ended on Thursday, and he had returned on Friday to 'put his classroom to bed' for the summer. Organizing textbooks, finalizing paper-work, and stacking tables and chairs were all part of the day

Rachel reached over and grabbed his hand. "Feel that?" she asked as she placed his open hand against her tummy.

Andrew smiled as he rolled over and pressed his head against Rachel's belly in the same spot his hand had been. "Hello in there," he called.

Rachel felt the baby kick again, and Andrew laughed as the thumping tickled his ear.

"Our baby is going to be perfect," Andrew said confidently.

"The perfect baby for us," Rachel said as she set the book she had been reading on the bedside table.

"Perfect," Andrew repeated. "How could he . . . she . . . whatever, be anything else, with you for a mother?"

"Dad ranks pretty high too," Rachel said.

Andrew smiled in acceptance of the compliment. "So have you given any more thought to a name?"

Rachel shrugged. "Not really. I feel kind of guilty, but I still like Melissa for a girl."

"What?" Andrew asked. "You feel guilty about not naming the baby after your mother?"

Rachel nodded. "When we thought we had lost mother, we said we would name the baby after her— assuming the baby was a girl."

"But we didn't lose her. Besides, we didn't tell anyone that's what we were planning to do," Andrew said.

"I guess you're right," she said. "I think I like Melissa for a girl and Andrew for a boy. Did you have any other ideas?"

"No, but it still feels funny to think of naming someone after me."

"Even your son?"

"Yeah, even my son. But I guess I'll get over it if that's what we decide on."

"There's no hurry," Rachel said.

"That's true, and maybe the baby won't look like an Andrew or a Melissa."

"Babies don't look like names," Rachel protested.

"Aren't names basically labels?" Andrew asked.

"Well, yes, but . . . "

"And don't we label things according to looks or actions or what they remind us of?" he argued.

"We name babies based on how we feel about them or the person we're naming them after," Rachel said.

"It's the same difference," Andrew said. "Either way, we may choose a completely different name once we see the baby."

"Okay," she said. "I can agree with that. We'll make our final decision after we see the baby."

"I suppose I should get going," Andrew said as he pulled the covers back. He sat up and swung his feet over the side of the bed.

"What are your plans for the day?" Rachel asked.

Andrew put on a pair of jeans and sorted through the shirts hanging in the closet. "I thought I would mow the lawn then go to the library," he said.

"The library?" she asked.

"Yeah, I need to finish some research," Andrew said as he took a shirt from a hanger and put it on.

"What research?" Rachel asked.

"Just some stuff I started working on last week when you were at Anna's."

"What kind of stuff?"

Andrew was reluctant to tell her what he had been searching for at the library, but he knew she wouldn't let up until he gave her a straight answer. Still, he thought he'd take his chances. "Nothing you'd be interested in," he said.

"Is there a reason you're giving such vague answers to my questions?"

He knew he'd been caught, but figured he'd make her work a little harder. "I'm looking for some information about a lady and her baby," he said.

"Do I know this woman?"

"I hope not—she's dead," he answered.

Rachel sat silently for several seconds. "Who is she?"

Andrew didn't dare face Rachel, so he continued rummaging in the closet for his favorite pair of sneakers. "I'm looking for information about Hank's wife," he said, bracing himself for Rachel's response.

Before responding, Rachel thought carefully about what her mother had told her after the baby shower. "Did you learn anything about her last week?" she asked.

"Look, I know . . . " Andrew stopped mid-sentence when Rachel's question registered in his mind. "What did you say?"

"I asked if you learned anything about her last week."

"Actually, I learned that they had a baby," he said, still shocked that she was expressing interest.

"Really?" she asked. "How did you learn that?"

"Believe it or not, the librarian told me. She remembered hearing stories as a young girl and said that they had a baby."

"If he killed his wife, what happened to the baby?" she asked.

"According to Edith, he is rumored to have killed his wife and baby."

"Rumored," Rachel said.

Andrew nodded. "Yeah, it is all rumor. So far, that's all we have to go by. Edith is helping me go through old editions of the local paper."

"I'm assuming that Edith is the librarian?" she said.

"Uh-huh," he confirmed.

Rachel smiled, but didn't say any more.

Andrew frowned. "Honey, I know you think I'm obsessed with Hank and his past. Just remember that I was interested from the first time I saw his house—before I knew anything of the rumors."

Rachel nodded. "That's true."

"Which is true?" Andrew asked. "The part about you thinking I'm obsessed or the last bit?"

"Both," Rachel said with a grin.

"Fair enough," he said as he put on his shoes. "But hear me out."

"Go ahead."

"I want to get to know Hank as a neighbor. I'm not really concerned about who he was or what he's done. If the rumors are true, that was a long time ago."

"Suppose you find the rumors are true. What then?" she questioned.

"What do you mean?"

"I mean, wouldn't you be a bit nervous living down the street from a murderer?"

Andrew scratched his head. "I thought you didn't believe the rumors."

"But what if they are true?" she asked.

He thought for a moment. "Well, I guess I'd be a little nervous, but I'm not sure that would be justified."

"Why not?" she asked.

"Well, because a lot of people have lived in this house since it was built thirty years ago, and I don't believe any of them had a problem. Why would things be any different with us living here?" Andrew asked.

"Because none of them pestered the poor man like the current occupants," Rachel teased.

"Okay, smarty," he said. "But it's like Edith said—if he's innocent, it's only right that everyone know the truth. If he's not, that *was* a long time ago."

"I guess that makes sense," Rachel admitted. "You go ahead with your research, but don't forget about me and our baby."

"You know I won't," he said. "So what did you have planned for the day?"

"Just the usual," she said. "You know, peeled grapes, bonbons . . . "

Andrew laughed. "In that case, I'll clean my teeth and be on my way. I'm hoping Edith has found something else."

Rachel smiled. "Should I start worrying about an obsession with Edith."

Andrew laughed. "You'd like Edith," he said. "She has a great sense of humor."

"I'd like to meet her, but I really don't want to spend all afternoon at the library," she said.

"From what she's told me, it sounds like she leads a pretty lonely life," Andrew said. "What if I invite her to dinner sometime?"

"That would be fine," Rachel said. "You could even invite her for tonight. Just be sure to let me know if she accepts the invitation."

"I will," Andrew said as he grabbed a baseball cap from the closet shelf. He put his head down by Rachel's tummy. "See you later, squirt," he said.

Andrew entered the building and looked for Edith. It appeared to be another slow Saturday at the library. After only a short search, he found Edith in a far corner helping a young girl choose some picture books.

"I'll be right with you," Edith mouthed from across the room.

Andrew stood at the front counter and looked through the books displayed on small wooden stands. He thumbed though a book titled *Mommy's Having a Baby*, and smiled as he looked at the illustrations of what the baby looked like as it grew. Lost in the daydream of holding the little bundle in his arms, he was completely unaware that Edith was now standing behind the counter.

"It is amazing, isn't it?" Edith said. She pointed at one of the illustrations in the book. "To think that we all looked like that at one time—I'm glad I can't remember."

Andrew chuckled. "I can't say I'd ever thought about that, Edith."

"How far along is your wife?" she asked.

"She's about seven months," Andrew said.

"Boy or girl?"

"Don't know," he answered.

"Good for you," Edith said. "Too many people these days like to open their presents before Christmas. Kind of takes all the fun out of it, don't you think?"

Andrew nodded. "That's what we think too."

"Good for you," Edith repeated. She reached underneath the counter and pulled out a piece of paper. "I have something to show you," she said as she laid the paper on the counter in front of Andrew.

He took the paper and turned it so that it was right

side up. "Doris Peterman," he read aloud from the photo-copied page of a newspaper. "Her obituary? When did you find this?"

"Last night after closing," she said. "I was beginning to think we weren't going to find anything, but here we are. It's not much, but it's a start."

"What do you mean it's not much? This is great."

"Read it," Edith said.

Andrew began reading aloud the words printed below the young women's photograph. "Doris Peterman, age 22, died in her home August 26th. She is survived by her husband." He turned the paper over as if expecting to find more on the back. "That's it?"

"I'm afraid so," Edith confirmed. "Not much to go on, but as I said, it's a start."

"I don't understand," Andrew said. "I read a lot of obituaries in the papers I went through, and they all contained more information than this. Why would this one be so sparse?"

"Obituaries are usually written by loved ones. If Hank wrote it, that may be all he wanted people to know," she suggested.

"Like he's trying to hide something?"

Edith laughed. "Slow down, cowboy—everyone knows he's a man of few words. Maybe that's all he had to say."

"But it did say she died in her home. Isn't that where the murder was supposed to have happened?"

"A lot of people died in their homes back then," she said. "Anyway, you sound like you hope he did kill her."

Andrew didn't say anything for a moment as he thought about Edith's statement. "I guess it does sound that way," he said. "I think I'm just caught up in the excitement of a good mystery."

"Then you should be just as happy if we find that he didn't kill anyone," Edith said. "From a different perspective, it's a positive thing that there is no mention of a baby in her obituary. There doesn't appear to be an obituary for a Baby Peterman."

"I guess you're right," Andrew agreed. "What year was this?"

"Oh no you don't. You're trying to trick me into telling you the year so you can determine that I'm in my late sixti . . . ." Edith covered her mouth with both hands as though she had accidentally revealed a great secret.

Andrew shook his head and laughed.

"1946," Edith said with a wink. "If there was foul play suspected, I would have expected to find an article about it in the same edition as the obituary."

"But it could be in subsequent editions," Andrew said.

"You're right. Why don't you go upstairs and see what you can find?" Edith suggested. "I brought a desk lamp so you can't claim to get another headache," she teased.

"Thank you, Edith," he whispered loudly as he headed around the corner.

Andrew was anxious to begin his search. Upstairs he found the edition of the paper containing the obituary, open flat on the big table. He carefully began reading headlines and turning pages of the following week's edition. The lamp Edith had provided made it much easier to read the old print, so Andrew soon found himself reading stories of interest, even though they were unrelated to his quest. He wasn't sure why, but he was particularly interested in a series of articles about one of the local citizens and his experiences while fighting in Europe during World War II.

It wasn't until his stomach growled that Andrew

realized he had worked through the entire afternoon. It would soon be 5:00 p.m. and time for the library to close. Even after all his hours of research, he still hadn't found anything more about Hank or Doris Peterman. He finished another paper and carefully set it aside. "Number ten," he said aloud as he picked up the next edition and began reading. Two-thirds of the way down page three, right below an article about a bank in Chicago opening the first ever drive-up teller windows, a headline caught his eye. "Rumors may be nothing more," he read aloud. "This is it."

Andrew picked up the paper and hurried downstairs. There was a line at the front counter where several people were waiting to check out their books before the library closed. After fifteen minutes, Edith finally served the last person.

"I think I've got it. There's an article here about her death." Andrew beamed with excitement as he handed the paper to Edith.

She took the paper from Andrew and walked past the counter to a photocopier in the corner. Carefully, she made a copy of the article. "Go put this back upstairs," she instructed.

Andrew wasted no time in taking the newspaper upstairs and returning to the front counter.

Edith shook her head and nodded as she read. "Very interesting," she said. "But don't you think it raises as many questions as it answers?"

"I guess, but now we know about the baby."

"Are you sure this is okay?" Edith asked as Andrew started the car and pulled away from the curb.

"She actually seemed excited when I called her."

"It really is very kind of you," Edith said. "It will be nice to spend an evening with someone for a change."

Andrew thought about how lonely Edith must feel. "Do you ever go out with friends or anything?" he asked.

"You know, it's a funny thing. My husband and I used to spend a lot of time with other couples. After he died and our friends started having children, I really didn't have anything in common with any of them."

Andrew nodded but couldn't think of the right words to say. He drove slowly as he made the left turn onto his street. "There it is," he said as he slowed the vehicle.

Edith looked out the window at the old house on the corner. "Why are you driving past it?" she asked.

"Not my house. Hank's."

Edith chuckled. "I knew what you meant. Could you stop?"

Andrew stopped the car. "Is something wrong?"

Edith shook her head. "You might as well back up," she said.

He backed up the car and stopped right in front of the house.

Without speaking, Edith got out of the car and walked up the sidewalk toward the front porch.

Andrew jumped out of the car and followed after her. He reached her just as she knocked on the front door. "Edith, what are you doing?" he asked.

"I'm going to see if I can get a better reception than you did," she said.

"He's not here," Andrew said.

"How do you know?" Edith questioned.

"Because his truck isn't here," he said.

"Oh—then I guess that changes things, doesn't it?"

Andrew laughed. "Yeah, I suppose it does."

Edith promptly turned around and headed back to the car. "Maybe you can bring me around some time when he is home," she said to Andrew as he climbed behind the wheel.

"Okay," he said slowly. He was still shocked by Edith's gutsy move. "Edith, I can't believe you just did that?"

"Can you think of a better time to do it?" she asked.

Andrew smiled. "When he's home."

Edith looked at Andrew and smiled. "So are you taking me home for dinner or not?"

Andrew chuckled as he started the car and headed home. "I have one more question," he said as he assisted Edith out of the car. "What would you have said to Hank if he had been home and had answered the door?"

Edith thought for a moment. "I don't know," she answered as she shrugged her shoulders and stepped inside through the door Andrew held open for her.

Rachel had heard them pull up and was at the door to meet them. "Hi, I'm Rachel and you must be Edith," she said with a smile.

"I am. And you must be Rachel." Edith reached up and gave Rachel a hug.

"I'm glad you were able to make it," Rachel said. She greeted Andrew with a hug and a kiss. "Andrew and I discussed it this morning and I hoped you would accept our invitation for this evening."

"You see, Edith" Andrew said, "I told you it was fine."

"I know you did," Edith said. "But I worry about troubling the two of you; especially with Rachel expecting and everything."

"I had to make dinner for Andrew and me anyway. One more person really isn't any more trouble," Rachel assured.

"I must admit I feel a little awkward," Edith said. "I don't visit others very often."

"Just make yourself at home," Rachel said. "Dinner is nearly ready. Andrew, why don't you seat Edith at the table, and I'll finish up in the kitchen?"

"Is there something I can do to help?" Edith asked.

Rachel shook her head. "I'm just about done," she said as she disappeared into the kitchen.

Andrew directed Edith to the card table in the dining area. He and Rachel hoped to one day have a formal dining set for the room, but for now, the card table, nicely set with a linen table cloth and stoneware, would have to do.

"She seems like a lovely girl, Andrew," Edith said.

"She certainly is," Andrew agreed. "Sometimes I think she's too good for me."

"I'm sure she is," Edith said with a grin. "But it's that same goodness that makes her keep you around."

Andrew laughed. "I'm sure you're right about that," he said as he pulled out a chair from the small table and assisted Edith into her seat.

"I hope you like pork chops, Edith," Rachel said as she entered the dining room with a plate full of meat and a bowl of mixed vegetables.

"They're one of my favorites," Edith said. She took the bowl from Rachel and placed it in the center of the table.

Rachel went back to the kitchen and returned with a bowl of mashed potatoes and a filled gravy boat.

"It all looks delicious," Edith said.

Everyone bowed their heads as Andrew gave thanks for the meal and the blessings of that day.

"Please help yourself, Edith," Rachel said when every-one had raised their heads.

"Thank you," Edith said as she placed a scoop of potatoes on her plate.

"Andrew has told me a few things about you, but maybe you'd like to share some more," Rachel said after everyone was served and had begun eating.

"Maybe you'd better tell me what Andrew's told you, so I can either defend myself or correct him," Edith said.

Rachel chuckled. "Well, he did tell me that you had a good sense of humor, and I can see he was right about that."

"Oh, it's not that good," Edith said. "It's just that life is full of funny things, but too many folks don't recognize them. I just point them out or highlight them, that's all. What else has he said?"

"Only that I would like you," she said.

"And do you?" Edith asked.

"Of course I do," Rachel answered.

"I see that you and Andrew both have a problem with snap judgments about people," Edith teased. "But, thank you."

Rachel smiled and nodded.

"Well, go on, Edith. Tell us more," Andrew prod-ded.

"There really isn't much to tell," Edith said. "I grew up here in town. My husband died over forty years ago, and I've worked at the library since then. That's about it."

"You must be a very strong woman," Rachel said. "That's a long time to be alone."

"What about other family?" Andrew asked.

Edith shook her head. "I was the youngest in my family and, let's just say I was a late-comer. My parents passed away about thirty years ago and the last of my three siblings died about ten years ago. My brother and sisters all lived out of state, so we rarely saw each other— and they were quite involved with their own children," she said. "But that's enough about me. How are you feeling, Rachel?"

"I'm doing very well, actually. Not much in the way of problems . . . at least as far as my health is concerned," she said quietly.

Andrew glared at Rachel and shook his head just slightly.

"Well, pregnancy certainly suites you," Edith said, noticing the gesture.

Rachel blushed. "Okay, that's enough about me. It must be Andrew's turn," she said.

"Everyone here knows more about me than they care to. But Edith and I have something to show you," Andrew said.

"What's that?" Rachel asked.

Andrew reached into his shirt pocket and pulled out two folded pieces of paper and handed them to Rachel.

Rachel unfolded them and read the first page. "Not much of an obituary," she said.

"That's what we thought," Edith said. "Obviously written by a man."

Edith's comment made Rachel chuckle.

Andrew just rolled his eyes and shook his head. "Read the next page," Andrew said.

She pulled the second paper from behind the other one and read aloud. "Rumors may be nothing more. After several months of speculation and unanswered questions regarding the death of 22-year-old Doris Peterman . . ."

chapter ❀ NINE

Rachel interrupted her reading. "I'm sorry, I guess I just assumed you wanted me to read the article out loud. Is that okay?" she asked Andrew and Edith.

"That's fine with me," Edith said.

"Me too," Andrew echoed, grateful that Rachel was showing some signs of interest in this mystery.

Rachel nodded, then began reading again:

> "Rumors may be nothing more. After several months of speculation and unanswered questions regarding the death of 22-year-old Doris Peterman and her newborn baby on August 26th, no further details have emerged, and the answers may forever remain a mystery, accord-

ing to Sheriff Mack Russell. The woman's husband, 24-year-old Henry Peterman, confessed to the murder of his wife and newborn child. Sheriff Russell was called to the Peterman home on the evening in question to investigate the death of Mrs. Peterman. Mr. Peterman was found sitting in a pool of blood, cradling his wife in his arms. He reportedly said, 'I didn't mean to kill them. This is my fault. I'm so sorry.' It wasn't until later that the sheriff discovered the corpse of a newborn child, umbilical cord still attached, under the woman's skirt.

"'When I first entered the house, Hank was bawling and kept apologizing for killing them, but he ain't said much since,' Russell said yesterday. Though Mr. Peterman confessed, doctors at County Hospital refuse to call either death a murder. They say Mrs. Peterman appears to have hemorrhaged to death. The baby most likely died prior to birth. 'There is no visible sign of a fight or anything else that points to a murder in this case,' a hospital spokesman said. 'An autopsy may change things, though,' he added.

"A court ordered autopsy is not possible since there is not enough evidence that a crime took place. Officials say the only way an autopsy could be performed is if Mr. Peterman authorizes one. In spite of many attempts by the sheriff and others to persuade Mr. Peterman to either explain his confession or authorize an autopsy, he continues to refuse. 'I'm so sorry,' is all he will say to investigators.

"With the confession as the only evidence to work with, prosecutors say Peterman will not be charged with murder. 'Unless Hank tells us what happened or lets us exhume the body and do an autopsy, all we have are rumors and speculation,' Russell said. 'As far as I'm concerned, the case is closed,' he added.

"Many townspeople, shocked by the tragedy, have joined in expressing their opinion of what happened. Some say Peterman was unhappy about the upcoming birth of his child and simply lashed out in a fit of rage. Others claim that, in spite of his reputation for being odd, he is not capable of murder. It appears, however, that for now, the truth will remain a mystery."

Rachel sat silently holding the papers in her hand.

"Well, what do you think?" Edith asked.

"I think it doesn't make a lot of sense," she said as she folded the papers and handed them back to Andrew.

"That's what we thought," Edith said.

"Edith, is the article correct about what people were saying at the time?" Rachel asked.

"I was just a teenager, so of course we latched on to the most dramatic, but everyone I ever talked to said he was guilty."

"I assume you believed them?" Rachel asked.

"Like I said, we believed the sensational. None of us knew the man, so we couldn't make an honest judgment."

"What were your parents saying about it?" Rachel asked.

Edith thought for a moment. "Not much really. They

said not to believe everything we heard."

"Then they thought he was innocent?" Rachel questioned.

Edith shrugged. "Who knows? But my parents generally had faith in others. I don't think they knew Mr. Peterman, so they probably tried to stay neutral about the whole thing."

Rachel nodded. "That was probably best."

Andrew had been sitting quietly since Rachel had finished reading the article. "What other explanation is there?" he asked.

"Explanation for what?" Edith asked in confusion.

"For the deaths," he answered. "If he didn't kill them, why would he confess?"

"Maybe she killed herself and he wanted to cover for her," Rachel suggested.

"That wouldn't explain the blood," Edith said.

"She's right," Andrew agreed. "According to the article, there was no sign of trauma."

"I guess you're right," Rachel admitted. "But I wasn't serious."

"Well, the whole thing is strange," Andrew said.

"I agree," Rachel said. "It's strange that we are even talking about something so gruesome when we could be visiting."

"You know, Andrew, Rachel is right," Edith said as she took the napkin from her lap and placed it on the table. She stood up and began clearing the dishes. "Let's talk about something more enjoyable while we clean up."

The three of them cleared the table and went into the kitchen to wash the dishes.

Edith made herself right at home. She found the dish soap under the sink, ran the water, and began washing dishes.

Rachel took a dish towel and dried the dishes while Andrew stood and stared out the window.

"Here," Rachel said as she handed Andrew a dried plate, "you can put the dishes away."

He smiled as he took the plate from her and placed it in the cupboard.

"You look a million miles away, Andrew," Edith observed. "What are you thinking about?"

"Nothing, really," he said.

"I'll bet you're thinking about that baby of yours," she said. "Aren't you getting excited?"

Andrew nodded. "Of course I am," he said.

"Oh come on. You can show more excitement than that," Edith said. "This is your first baby."

Rachel stopped what she was doing and turned to look at Andrew.

Andrew squirmed uncomfortably. "You enjoy putting me on the spot, don't you, Edith," he said.

"Yep," she said with a chuckle.

Andrew walked over and wrapped his arms around Rachel. "I know I haven't always shown a lot of enthusiasm, but this really is the best thing that's ever happened to us, and I can't wait," he said towards Rachel's tummy.

Rachel smiled as she ran her fingers through Andrew's hair. "I'm afraid you'll have to wait," she said.

Edith drained the water from the sink and turned around. She grinned as she looked at Andrew rubbing Rachel's abdomen. "Rachel, I owe you an apology."

"Apology for what, Edith?" she asked.

"For encouraging your husband in his super sleuthing," she said. "This whole thing with the Petermans could have waited until after your baby was born."

"Don't worry about it," Rachel said.

"I won't worry. But neither will I continue to encourage Sherlock Holmes here."

Andrew shook his head and laughed.

"I really don't mind—as long as Andrew remembers that the baby and I come first."

"I promised you this morning that I would," Andrew said. "And I still mean it."

"That's good enough for me," Edith said. "But we'll keep our investigations to a minimum, won't we Sherlock?"

"We certainly will, Watson," he said with a nod.

"Well, I do have a question for the two of you," Edith said. "Even though you don't want to know whether you're getting a boy or a girl, do you have a preference?"

"I don't," Rachel said with a smile.

"Me either," Andrew said, "as long as it's a healthy baby."

"I'm sure there's nothing to worry about there," Edith said.

Rachel's smile waned as she tipped her head and stared at the floor.

Edith was quick to pick up on the sudden change in mood. She turned and walked toward the door. "Well, I hate to eat and run, but as I told Andrew when I agreed to join you for dinner, I have some things at home that require my attention. Andrew, would you mind running me home now?"

"No problem," he said.

"I wish you didn't have to go," Rachel said. "You will join us again sometime, won't you?"

"Thank you," Edith said. "I'd like that very much."

"We'll get with you soon so we can set another date," Rachel said.

"That will be fine. I'll look forward to hearing from

you," Edith replied. "Come on, Andrew, I'm not getting any younger."

"See you in a few minutes," Andrew said to Rachel as he gave her a quick kiss and followed after Edith. "I won't be long," he called over his shoulder as he left through the front door. He hurried to the car, where Edith was already sitting in the passenger seat. He started the car and backed out of the driveway.

Edith watched Andrew closely as they drove down the street and past the Peterman home. His eyes veered slightly to the left as they neared the house.

"Looking at anything in particular?" Edith asked.

"What are you referring to?" Andrew asked.

"Your eyes were glued to that house," she said.

"They were not," Andrew said in disbelief.

"They most certainly were," Edith asserted. "I was afraid you were going to keep looking as we turned the corner and that your head would spin completely off your neck."

"I believe you're exaggerating a bit," he said.

"Not much," she mumbled.

Andrew laughed.

"Seriously, Andrew, I'm afraid I'm guilty of aiding you in neglecting what should be your highest priority."

"What do you mean?" he asked. "I spend most of my time at home with Rachel, especially in the summer."

"Forgive me for saying so, but just because you are in the house, it doesn't mean that you are home."

"I'm afraid I don't follow you," he said.

Edith sighed. "You're dumber than I thought."

"Hey, I heard that," Andrew said with a chuckle.

"I intended you to hear it," she said with a grin. "Look, it may not be my place to say anything, but my observation is that you're putting too much energy into figuring out what happened in your neighbor's house over fifty years ago and not enough energy into figuring out what's happening in your own house right now."

"I'm well aware of what's going on in my home," he defended.

"Are you, Andrew?" Edith asked.

Andrew wasn't sure how to respond. He fidgeted nervously in his seat.

"If it's none of my business, just tell me, but I sense that Rachel is very nervous about having this baby."

"How can you get all of that from just one evening with her?" Andrew asked.

"You're a math teacher, aren't you? You should know that you can't solve a problem using only a few of the factors."

"What else have you picked up on?" he asked.

"Well, it seemed quite obvious to me that Rachel really has very little interest in the Petermans, but plays along to keep you happy. Am I right?"

"Possibly," he said quietly.

"She even said tonight that she didn't mind if you pursued your interest as long as you didn't forget that she and the baby come first," Edith said.

"I'm trying to put her first," Andrew said. "Really, I am."

Edith shook her head and sighed. "Andrew, listen to what you just said. You're *trying* to put her first. And what about the baby?"

"I figure the baby's included when I put Rachel first," he said.

"There's a little, separate person there," Edith said. "Rachel and the baby aren't the same person. The sooner you understand that, the better things will be for all of you."

Andrew pulled into the driveway at Edith's house, which was just a block from the library. He put the car into park and turned off the engine. He sat quietly, waiting for Edith to continue.

"Do you know what's bothering Rachel?" she asked.

"I think I have a pretty good idea," Andrew said.

"Do you want to tell me about it?" Edith asked.

Andrew sighed deeply as he turned and looked out the window. "There's a slightly higher than usual chance that the baby will be born with Down syndrome," he said. "But I'm sure things will be fine."

"Ahhh," Edith said, as she contemplated Andrew's response. "You hope things will be fine, but the baby could still be born with Down syndrome."

"That's exactly what Rachel said."

Edith reached over and patted Andrew on the leg. "Andrew, I like you a lot and it's been fun looking for clues about your neighbor, but you need to focus on your family." She paused, trying to find the right words. "Take it from an old lady who has become an expert in observation. It seems to me that you are trying to stay busy and not think too much about how things might be when the baby is born. Rachel doesn't have the luxury of those kinds of distractions. The baby is with her all the time, and it's probably hard for her to think about anything else. She may even think that the situation could somehow be her fault."

Andrew was very quiet. Edith's words struck a nerve and made sense at the same time. He wasn't sure how to respond.

Noting Andrew's silence, Edith continued. "We can work on Peterman later. Who knows? Maybe he'll walk right up to you some day and tell you all about it."

"That'll be the day," Andrew chuckled.

"Promise me that you'll give this some thought," Edith insisted.

"I promise," Andrew whispered. "Thank you, Edith."

"My pleasure," she said as she opened the door and got out of the car, waving as she went inside.

Andrew drove home slower than usual. He knew that Edith was probably right, but it bothered him that he may have been so blind to Rachel's needs. He'd also never let himself admit the real possibility that the baby could be born with Down syndrome.

As he turned the corner onto their street, he did his best not to pay any attention to Hank's house, but as was often the case, the old truck was there in the yard and the driver's door was wide open. Andrew stopped and, as he had done several times over the past weeks, went up and closed the truck door. Normally he was tempted to knock at the front door, just to see if Hank would answer. Instead he got back in the car and drove home.

Andrew stepped inside and found Rachel rocking back-and-forth in the rocking chair. Without saying anything, he went over and sat down on the floor in front of her. He lifted her feet onto his lap and rubbed them gently.

Rachel smiled as she looked into her husband's eyes. "What's that for?" she asked.

"For you," Andrew said. "And for the baby."

chapter TEN

"Ouch," Rachel groaned as she put her hand on her side and stood up. She walked around the bed to answer the ringing telephone. "Hello."

"How are you this morning?" Anna asked.

"Better now that I know you're still around," Rachel said. "I was beginning to wonder if you'd forgotten about me."

Anna laughed. "Sorry, it's been crazy at the store and . . . well—I guess that's my only excuse."

Rachel put a pillow against the headboard and laid one underneath her feet. She settled in for what she knew was likely to be a long conversation with her twin sister. "We've got a lot of catching up to do," she said into the receiver.

"I know we do," Anna agreed. "So how have you been feeling?"

"Not too bad. My back still aches most of the time, and I'm getting a little tired of the swollen ankles," Rachel said.

"But doesn't it feel good to know that you only have a few days left?" Anna asked.

"Feel good?" Rachel echoed. "Nothing feels good right know, but it is good to know that there's a light at the end of the tunnel."

Anna chuckled. "And how are you holding up in this heat?"

"I've heard that women put on an average of twenty pounds with pregnancy, but I swear I've put on twenty degrees," Rachel replied.

"That bad, huh?"

"Oh, I suppose it's not quite that bad," Rachel admitted. She winced as her abdominal muscles tightened, then relaxed.

"What else have you been up to besides getting ready for the baby?" Anna asked.

"Just now, I was rearranging the contents of my drawers so that one will be available for diapers and other things—you know, the necessities for those nighttime feeding sessions," Rachel said.

"Sounds like fun," Anna said with a giggle.

"You'll have your chance some day," Rachel said. "Then we'll see who's laughing."

"It's just funny to hear that you're doing all these domestic things."

"Well, it's not like I have a choice, is it?"

"I suppose you're right," Anna said. "What's Andrew doing today?"

"He's . . . "

"Hey," Anna interrupted, "that reminds me. Last time we talked, you never got to tell me how things went when you visited his parents in June."

"No, I guess I didn't," Rachel said, relieved that she could momentarily avoid the topic of Andrew's library visits. "It went quite well, really."

"What did you do?"

"Mostly visited," Rachel said. "Brenda was home for the summer, so this is the first time all four of them have been together since our visit before Christmas. I spent a lot of time with Brenda and her mom, and Andrew spent most of his time at the store with his dad."

"How's Andrew's mother doing?"

"Okay, I suppose," Rachel answered. "Andrew said he can't remember a time when she wasn't sick."

"That must get pretty discouraging for her," Anna said.

"I'm sure it does, but she seems to handle it well," Rachel said. "Rob's very supportive and Sandra seems to have a positive attitude, even when you know she's not feeling well."

"Do they know what's wrong?" Anna asked.

"I don't think they're really sure," Rachel said. "Sandra told me she was healthy until she became pregnant with Andrew, and then everything seemed to fall apart. The doctor suggested that another pregnancy might straighten things out for her. It took six years for her get pregnant again. Then they were afraid they were going to lose her when Brenda was born."

"Hmmm," Anna said. "So Andrew's the problem?" she teased.

Rachel laughed. "That's what I tell him."

"How is Andrew doing?"

"He's fine," Rachel said.

"You know what I mean," Anna said. "How is he dealing with things?"

"He's actually doing very well," Rachel said. "Edith, the lady I told you about . . . "

"The librarian?"

"That's her," Rachel confirmed. "She has a way with him. She told him he needed to be more thoughtful of my needs, and since then he's really been trying."

"No more obsessing about your neighbor?" Anna asked.

"He still goes down and knocks on the door occasionally. Sometimes he even takes a plate of cookies or a fresh loaf of bread—not that it makes any difference." Rachel said.

"The old man still won't come to the door?" Anna asked.

"No," Rachel said. "But Andrew doesn't really say much about him or the house anymore."

"Does he say much about the baby?" Anna asked.

"He talks a lot about the baby. But if I say anything about the possibility of Down syndrome, he still changes the subject," Rachel said. "I wish he would do more to prepare himself, just in case. I've been doing some reading about Down's and I feel like I'm ready to accept the diagnosis if necessary. Unfortunately, I don't know that he will be."

"So what's your biggest fear?" Anna asked.

"That I'm not ready for all the medical conditions that can accompany Down's," Rachel said. "And . . . I'm worried about Andrew, like I said."

"Well, don't worry too much," Anna said. "With me, Mom, and Edith behind both of you, I'm sure things will be fine."

Rachel chuckled. "I'm sure you're right."

"Are you having any contractions yet?" Anna asked.

"Quite a few," Rachel said. "They're just not very regular yet."

"Weren't you at the doctor's yesterday?" Anna asked.

"Uh-huh," Rachel confirmed.

"What did he have to say?"

"He says it could happen any time, but probably within a week."

"So the baby could come before Andrew goes back to work on Wednesday?"

"I'm pretty sure it will," Rachel said.

"Are his parents planning on coming up when the baby's born?" Anna asked.

"No," Rachel responded. "I'm sure Sandra would be willing, even though I'm sure she doesn't feel up to traveling. But there's no way Rob could leave the store."

"Is his the only grocery store down there?" Anna asked.

"The only one within about a hundred miles," Rachel said. "But besides that, his only employees are a couple of high school kids. There would be no one to run the business."

"I guess that makes sense," Anna said. "When will they get to see the baby?"

"We'll send pictures, of course, but they're hoping to make it up here for Thanksgiving. It's too bad they have to wait so long to see their first grandchild, but some things can't be helped," Rachel said. "You just learn to live with them."

"Learn to live with what?" Andrew asked.

Rachel hadn't heard Andrew come in and was startled by his voice. "Hang on a minute, Anna. Andrew just came in," she said.

"I've really got to be going anyway," Anna said. "I'll talk to you again next week. You be sure and let me know if anything's happening before then."

"You know I will," Rachel said.

"Okay. Good-bye, and tell Andrew 'hi' for me," Anna requested.

"All right, I'll talk to you later. Bye," Rachel said as she hung up the telephone. She looked up at Andrew who was now standing beside the bed. "Finished with the lawn?"

"Not quite, but the mower's run out of gas. I'm going to run downtown and get some," Andrew said. "Do you want to come, or do you need anything?"

"I don't think so," Rachel said. "I'll just finish rearranging the drawers."

"Okay, I shouldn't be long," Andrew said, and gave Rachel a kiss before leaving. Once outside, he retrieved a small gas can from the detached garage on the corner of their property. The old wooden building sat at the end of the driveway and had two heavy swinging doors. Andrew had never dared park the car inside, partly because of the rickety old wooden floor, but mostly because he wasn't sure it was even wide enough to fit a vehicle.

After putting the can in the trunk of the car, Andrew backed out of the driveway and headed down the street. As he approached the corner, something struck him as odd. It only took a few seconds for him to realize that it was nearly midday and the old pickup was still parked at the side of Hank's house. Hank was never at home after 7:00 a.m.

Though they had never talked since their first brief meeting, Andrew felt a real sense of duty in watching out for his neighbor. He parked the car in front of the old house and got out to investigate. Though he knew

Hank wouldn't answer, even if he was home, Andrew knocked on the front door. When there was nothing but extended silence, he moved over and looked through the large window. He could see little through the hazy glass, but there didn't appear to be anyone in the front room. Moving to the other end of the porch, he looked through a smaller window into the kitchen. He could see enough to determine that the room was not occupied, so he returned to his car and continued toward his original destination.

As he drove to the gas station, Andrew wondered if he should have walked around the house and looked in the other windows. He thought he could remember another door on the side of the house, near the back. Perhaps he should have knocked on it.

On the way home, Andrew stopped at the only stop light in town. He was still thinking about Hank and hoped he was okay. He was surprised when the man in car behind him began honking his horn and was embarrassed when he looked up to see the light change from yellow to red. Making sure to pay attention, Andrew waited for the light to change from red to green again. Just then, the passenger door of his car opened and someone climbed inside.

Andrew turned his head slowly and gasped when he saw Hank seated next to him. "It's you," he stammered.

"Expecting someone else?" the man asked gruffly.

"Yes . . . I mean, no . . . I mean . . . I wasn't expecting anyone," Andrew managed to say.

"Then why didn't you go?" he asked.

"The light was red," Andrew answered.

"You sat through a green light," Hank said.

The blaring horn from the car behind interrupted the discussion. Andrew looked up just in time to see the light turn from green to yellow again. Quickly accelerating through the intersection before the light turned red once more, he looked in his rearview mirror and caught the reflection of the angry driver behind him. Andrew was grateful the man turned the corner rather than following him.

"So Hank, or would you rather I call you Mr. Peterman?" Andrew asked.

"No matter," Hank mumbled.

"I've been trying to meet you for months and you've acted like that was the last thing you wanted. So why now?" Andrew asked, still shocked by the sudden appearance of his elusive neighbor.

"Thought you were waiting for me," Hank said, noting Andrew's discomfort. "If I was mistaken, you can drop me off right here."

At first, Andrew was confused, but realized that Hank must have been watching him when he sat through the first green light at the intersection and assumed Andrew was waiting to give him a ride. "No, actually, I was waiting for you," Andrew said in order to avoid embarrassing Hank, not to mention himself. "So why aren't you driving your truck?"

Hank continued staring straight ahead, as he had done since he got in the car. "Won't start," he said.

Andrew grew excited as he realized that after several months of being unable to even talk to Hank, Hank was now sitting right next to him. "Are you coming from work?"

Hank nodded again.

"What line of work are you in?" Andrew asked.

Hank looked down at his bib overalls and dust covered boots, then turned his head and glared at Andrew as if to say, "are you stupid?"

Andrew wasn't sure what to say, so he didn't say anything for a while. Then he figured it would be a waste of what little time he had for asking questions. "I'm not sure if you remember me, but I'm your neighbor."

Hank gave the same glare as before.

"Of course you remember," Andrew said. "You know, my wife and I would love to have you join us for dinner sometime."

The continued silence made Andrew wonder if he had made a mistake in trying to hold this conversation with Hank. Still, Andrew forged ahead, hoping for some kind of breakthrough.

"My name is Andrew," he offered.

Once again, Hank turned and glared, but this time he spoke. "I know. You told me."

Andrew couldn't recall telling Hank his name. He thought for a moment before remembering the first time he had ventured to Hank's home. He had, indeed, introduced himself to Hank, just before getting the door slammed in his face. "So I did," he mumbled.

The two men were silent as they turned onto their street. Andrew stopped the car in front of Hank's house. "Can I help you with your truck?"

"You a mechanic?" Hank asked.

"No. I'm a math teacher, but I'm quite handy," Andrew said proudly.

"No thanks," Hank said as he opened the door and got out of the car.

Ignoring Hank's refusal, Andrew turned off the car and got out. Hank headed for the house, but Andrew went to the old pickup and climbed in the driver's seat and found the keys in the ignition. Andrew turned the key and got no response. He got out, went to the front of the truck, and lifted the hood.

Hank had turned around and was now standing by Andrew.

Andrew checked the connections on the battery, and pushed on the coil and spark plug wires to make sure they were snug. "It acts like your battery," Andrew said.

"It is my battery," Hank said, annoyed.

"You knew?" Andrew asked.

Hank snorted.

"Then why did . . . never mind," Andrew said. "So do you think it's bad, or does it just need to be charged?"

"Just charging," Hank replied.

"I've got some jumper cables if you want to try jumping it," Andrew offered.

Hank just shrugged, so Andrew hurried to his car before Hank could refuse his help again. Andrew pulled the car beside the truck and unlatched the hood. He was surprised when Hank actually lifted the hood while waiting for Andrew to get the jumper cables from the trunk. They attached the cables to the appropriate posts of the two batteries.

"Give it a try," Andrew said.

Hank stepped over the cables and got in his truck. He turned the key and after a few attempts, the engine began to roar.

Andrew got out and disconnected the cables. As he was putting down the hood of the truck, he thought he detected the hint of a smile on Hank's face. "I suppose you'll want to run the engine for a while, you know, to give the battery a chance to charge," Andrew said.

Hank nodded.

"Well, I'd better get home," Andrew said. He extended his right hand to Hank.

Hank looked down at Andrew's hand and hesitantly grasped it with his.

Andrew smiled as he started back toward his car.

"I'm a farmer," Hank volunteered.

Andrew stopped and turned, surprised at Hank's voluntary comment. He looked at Hank and nodded. "I probably should have realized that," he said.

"Probably," Hank said. "Thanks," he added.

"You're welcome," Andrew said. "And the invitation for dinner still stands."

True to form, Hank simply nodded.

Andrew could hardly wait to get home and tell Rachel about Hank. He waved as he backed onto the street and drove away from Hank's place. At the end of the street, he pulled into his driveway. He took the gasoline can from the trunk of the car and put it in the old garage before hurrying inside.

"You'll never guess what just happened to me," he said to Rachel.

Rachel was sitting in the rocking chair, folding laundry. "You had a flat tire?"

"No," he said with a smile.

"Okay, you went to the library and found out more about the Petermans."

"Even better than that," Andrew said. "I just had an actual conversation with Hank Peterman."

"You're kidding," Rachel said in disbelief.

"I've never been more serious," he said, before relating the whole story to Rachel.

"That's great," Rachel said when he'd finished. "I'd love to have him join us for dinner. He sounds like a very nice man."

"He is," Andrew said. "But now that we're on speaking terms, we should be able to clear up this mystery."

"I'm sure you're right," Rachel said. "Now I have some exciting news for you."

"Do I have to guess?" Andrew asked.

Rachel chuckled. "We're having a baby," she said.

"Yeah, and . . . " Andrew coaxed.

"And I think we're having it real soon."

"What do you mean?" Andrew asked excitedly. "Are you in labor?"

Rachel grimaced as another contraction started. "My contractions are coming regularly and are about ten minutes apart," she said as the contraction subsided.

Andrew's eyes grew wide. "Don't we need to get to the hospital or something?" he asked.

"Not yet," Rachel said. "I talked to Dr. Jeffery about a half hour ago. He said it could still be several hours, but that I should contact him when the contractions are about five to seven minutes apart. He'll have us go to the hospital then."

"So what do we do in the mean time?" Andrew asked.

"Well, you can go finish mowing the lawn. When I'm done here, I'll make dinner," she said.

"Right," Andrew said as he hurried for the front door. "Oh," he said as he turned and gave Rachel a kiss. "I'll hurry."

Rachel laughed. "Calm down, Andrew. Things won't progress any faster just because you're hurrying."

"Aren't you scared, or excited, or something?" Andrew asked.

Rachel smiled. "I was. But I called Mom too."

"Right," he said as he hurried outside.

Andrew slept through Rachel's tossing and turning, but she finally got out of bed to walk around at about 4:00 a.m. She found that walking seemed to ease the pain from the contractions. The labor pains were now about eight minutes apart, but Rachel decided she'd let Andrew sleep as long as he could. She packed a bag with a few essentials, and then took a hot bath for about an hour.

At 5:30 a.m, the contractions were coming every seven minutes, so Rachel decided to call Dr. Jeffery. He instructed her to meet him at the hospital, so she woke Andrew. She giggled as she watched him fumbling around in the closet, looking for a pair of shoes. In the end, she found them for him.

They arrived at the hospital and Dr. Jeffery met them in the Labor and Delivery unit. After the nurses got Rachel settled in, the doctor examined her.

"You're close, Rachel," Dr. Jeffery announced. "If you continue at this rate, I think you could have a baby within a few hours."

Andrew and Rachel looked at each other and smiled.

"So now what?" Andrew asked.

"Well, the nurses will need to put in an I.V. and finish getting Rachel admitted. You just help her with the breathing techniques the nurses will show her," the doctor said. "I'll come back in about an hour to see how things are progressing."

"Thanks, Dr. Jeffery," Rachel said.

He patted Rachel's hand. "You're welcome," he said. "Now try to stay as relaxed as you can and remember not to push until we tell you to."

Rachel nodded.

Andrew paced nervously as the nursing staff finished the admitting paperwork and placed an I.V. in Rachel's left hand. He watched the two waveforms on the monitor beside the bed, but had no idea what he was looking for. When the nurses finished, he sat down next to the bed and took Rachel's hand. "Did you think this day would ever come?" he asked.

"I was beginning to wonder," she said.

Andrew reached up and pushed the hair off Rachel's forehead. "I love you so much," he said.

"I love you too, honey," she said.

"Can I do anything for you?" he asked.

"You should probably call Mom and let her know we're here," Rachel suggested. "Do you think you should call your parents?"

Andrew shook his head and picked up the phone. "I told them we'd call when the baby's here."

As Rachel waited for Andrew to finish his conversation with her mother, she considered how their lives were about to change forever. She was sure she couldn't completely comprehend the changes that were about to occur, but was confident that they could get through them together.

When Dr. Jeffery returned, he was pleased to discover that things had progressed nicely. He instructed the nurses to get ready to deliver a baby. Because of his concerns about the baby, he had called one of his colleagues to assist.

Dr. Flanders arrived at the same time as several other people in surgical scrubs.

"Are all these people necessary?" Andrew asked.

"In light of the possibilities, we want to be prepared," Dr. Jeffery said.

Andrew nodded, but didn't say anything. He felt a bit nervous, but didn't want Rachel to know. He moved to the head of the bed and squeezed her hand.

Rachel was having a hard time resisting the urge to

push, in spite of her controlled breathing. She was grateful when the drapes were in place and the doctor finally gave her permission to bear down.

"Andrew, do you want to come down here so you can see?" Dr. Jeffery asked.

Andrew looked at Rachel, who nodded her approval. He let go of her hand and moved to the foot of the bed where he could watch what was happening.

After about fifteen minutes of pushing, the doctor announced that he could see the head. "Okay, Rachel, give me a big push," he instructed.

Rachel pushed with everything she had. Andrew grinned from ear-to-ear as the baby's head emerged.

"One more big one, Rachel, and I think we'll have this baby out," Dr. Jeffery said.

Again, Rachel gave it her all. Dr. Jeffery turned the baby's shoulders slightly, and the rest of the body appeared.

Dr. Jeffery turned to Dr. Flanders and nodded. A nurse handed Dr. Jeffery two clamps, which he placed on the umbilical cord, about an inch apart. Another nurse cut the cord and handed the baby to Dr. Flanders, who quickly joined the others in the corner of the room.

"You have a little girl," Dr. Jeffery announced.

Andrew just stood where he was, not knowing whether to direct his attention to Rachel or the baby. There seemed to be an unusual amount of activity in the corner with Dr. Flanders, so he moved up by Rachel's head. "We have a little girl," he whispered into her ear. He pushed the perspiration-soaked hair from her forehead and kissed her.

"Is everything okay?" Rachel asked when she didn't hear the baby cry.

"Everything looked fine on the monitor during delivery," the doctor said. "The baby just needs a little stimulation."

As Dr. Jeffery finished his explanation, the cry of a newborn baby echoed from the corner of the room. After a minute or so, a nurse wrapped the baby in a blanket and brought her to Rachel.

Rachel looked at the little bundle in her arms and started crying. "Isn't she beautiful," she said through the tears.

Andrew just nodded.

chapter ✺ ELEVEN

Rachel reached down inside the blanket and took her baby's hand between her thumb and forefinger. She hoped the baby would grip her finger, but wasn't too disappointed when she didn't. "She doesn't look like a Melissa, does she?" she asked.

Andrew was looking at the baby, but appeared to be miles away.

"Andrew?"

He looked at Rachel. "Huh? Oh . . . uh, yeah, Melissa is fine."

"I just said, she doesn't look like a Melissa. What do you think?"

Andrew shrugged. "I don't know. I guess I hadn't really thought about it."

"What's wrong?" Rachel asked.

"Nothing."

"Okay," Rachel said, though she wasn't convinced. "Shouldn't you call our parents?"

Andrew shook his head.

Rachel looked down at the peacefully sleeping bundle in her arms. She tucked the baby's hand back under the blanket. "Don't you think they deserve to know about their beautiful new granddaughter?"

"Dr. Jeffery said he would like to speak to us after he cleaned up," he answered as he moved his chair closer to the hospital bed and took Rachel's hand in his. "You know what he wants to talk to us about, don't you?"

Rachel squeezed his hand. "Yes, but it doesn't matter. She's here, she's ours, and she's obviously healthy."

Andrew looked down at the small nose and slightly slanted eyes. "Aren't you scared?"

"Of course I'm scared," she said. "But look at her . . ."

"I know," Andrew interrupted. "She's beautiful."

"She's beautiful," Rachel repeated. "Since she's definitely not a Melissa, what do you think we should call her?"

Andrew just shook his head.

"Come on," Rachel said. "Help me out here."

"I don't know what you want me to do."

"Help me figure out a name for this little bundle of joy. . . . That's it," Rachel said, excitedly.

"What's it?" he asked.

"Joy. We should name her Joy."

Andrew looked at the baby, then at Rachel. He smiled and nodded his approval.

"Joy it is," Rachel said as Dr. Jeffery came into the room.

"Sounds like there's a lot of joy in here," Dr. Jeffery said with a chuckle.

"What do you think?" Rachel asked as she propped the baby up. "Don't you think Joy suits her?"

Dr. Jeffery smiled. "I think that's the perfect name," he said as he pulled a chair next to Andrew's and sat down.

Andrew grew anxious as the doctor stared at him, at Rachel, at the baby, and back at him again. "So what did you want to see us about, Dr. Jeffery?" he asked.

"I'll get right to the point," he said. "The preliminary indicators are that your baby does have Down syndrome. She presented like a Down's baby—a little flaccid, and we had to stimulate her a bit more than usual to get her breathing.

"What else?" Rachel asked.

"You may have noticed some of the physical features, like the slightly slanted eyes, a flatter facial profile with a small, slightly depressed nose." He reached over and uncovered Joy's hand. "If you look here, you'll see that the palm has only one single crease and her little finger only has one joint."

"So basically, you know she has it?" Andrew questioned.

Dr. Jeffery nodded. "We'll need to do a test to make a formal diagnosis, but yes, Andrew, she has Down syndrome."

Andrew bit his lower lip as he fought back tears. Though he had known what Dr. Jeffery was going to tell them, somehow hearing him say the words made it sink in.

"There are other things we'll need to test her for," Dr. Jeffery continued.

"You mean like the heart condition that showed up on the ultrasound?" Rachel asked.

"Exactly, although Dr. Flanders said he isn't sure we'll find anything."

"What do you mean?" she asked.

"If you remember, the ultrasound showed a small opening between the upper chambers of the heart. Sometimes, if the opening is small enough, it closes on its own."

"So she wouldn't need surgery?" Rachel asked.

"That's right," Dr. Jeffery said. "As long as she's doing this well, we'll just watch her for now and schedule an echocardiogram tomorrow to see for sure."

"That sounds reasonable." Rachel looked over at her husband, who was still struggling to control his emotions.

Andrew nodded, but didn't speak.

"I'll arrange for the hospital social worker to meet with the two of you as well," the doctor said. "She can direct you to community resources and other services that can give you the support you'll need."

"That would be great," Rachel said. "Thank you."

"You're welcome," Dr. Jeffery responded. "Now, I'll leave the three of you alone so you can get acquainted."

Rachel reached over with her free hand and placed it on Andrew's shoulder. "Are you all right?" she asked.

"I thought you said you were scared," Andrew responded hesitantly.

"I am."

"Then maybe I'm just a wimp," he suggested as he lowered his eyes to the floor.

"Because the news made you get emotional?" Rachel asked.

"You seemed to handle it okay."

Rachel gently touched Andrew's cheek with her hand. "That's because it wasn't news to me," she said softly.

Andrew lifted his head. "You've known all along, haven't you?"

Rachel tightened her lips and nodded.

"And I was too foolish to see it," he said.

"Or maybe too frightened," she suggested.

Andrew sighed. "We'd better make some phone calls." He picked up the telephone and dialed Martha's number. He held the receiver a little further from his ear than usual, so that Rachel could hear both sides of the conversation. "Hi, Mom, this is Andrew," he said when Martha answered the phone.

"Well . . . ?" Martha asked in anticipation.

"You have another grandchild," he announced.

"All right, smarty pants," Martha said impatiently. "Boy or girl?"

Andrew chuckled. "You have another granddaughter."

Rachel smiled as she heard her mother's scream over the telephone.

"And how are Mom and the baby?" Martha asked.

"They're fine," he said.

"So how big? Have you chosen a name?"

"She is six pounds, eight ounces, and eighteen inches long," he said.

"And the name?" Martha coaxed.

"Joy," he said.

"Oh," Martha squealed. "Everyone should have a little Joy in their lives."

Andrew and Rachel both chuckled.

"Yes, and now we do," Andrew said.

"Little Joy," Martha affectionately repeated. "Well, I won't keep you, but give my love to the girls and don't worry about calling the others; I'll take care of that."

"That would be great, thank you," he said.

"Ask Rachel if she thinks she will feel up to a visit this afternoon."

Rachel nodded.

"She said that would be fine," Andrew said.

"Then I'll plan on coming over after church," she said.

"Great," Andrew said.

"Good-bye and congratulations," Martha said.

"Bye," Andrew said and then hung up the telephone.

"Don't you think you should have said more?" Rachel asked.

"Why?" he asked.

"I just thought it might have been nice to let her know," Rachel said.

"What was I supposed to say? By the way Mom, she's got Down syndrome," he asked sarcastically.

"There's no need to get upset," Rachel said calmly.

"Everyone will know soon enough. I don't think we need to tell anyone."

Rachel nodded, knowing it would be better not to push Andrew at the moment.

Andrew picked up the telephone again and dialed his parent's number into the keypad. "Did you want to listen in?" he asked.

"Sure," Rachel said.

Once again, he leaned forward in the chair and held the earpiece away from his ear so Rachel could hear both ends of the conversation.

"Hi, Dad," Andrew said when his father answered the phone. "Just thought you'd like to know that you have a granddaughter."

"Congratulations, son," he said. "Sandra, they have a girl," they could hear him say in the background. "Mom wants to know how everyone is doing."

"They're fine," Andrew said.

"Mom wants to know . . . oh here, I'll just give her

the phone so she can ask for herself," Rob said.

"Hello," Sandra said.

"Hi, Mom. How are you feeling?"

"Never mind how I'm feeling," Sandra said impatiently. "How big is the baby?"

"She's six pounds, eight ounces, and eighteen inches," he said.

"Have you decided on a name?"

"Joy," Andrew said.

"Oh, that's a lovely name. Joy Ingram. I like that," Sandra said. "So describe her to me."

"Um . . ." Andrew stammered as he looked at Rachel, hoping she would come to his rescue.

Rachel's only offer of help was a smug grin. "You're the one who has this all figured out," she whispered.

"Uh . . . well, she's small and has a little dark hair," he said.

"Tell me about her eyes," Sandra requested.

"Her eyes?" Andrew repeated.

"Yes, her eyes. You know, the things that separate her cheeks from her forehead?"

"Uh, yeah . . . well . . ." Andrew stammered.

"Oh good grief, son. Are her eyes showing any color yet?"

"They're brownish, I think," Andrew quickly offered in relief.

"Now, that wasn't so hard, was it?" Sandra asked.

Andrew didn't answer.

"Never mind. Now you be sure to send us some pictures," she requested.

"Sure thing, Mom," Andrew said.

"Hopefully we'll see you at Thanksgiving—if we're still invited."

"Of course you are," he affirmed.

"Tell Rachel we're proud of her and give Joy a kiss for us."

"I'll do it," Andrew assured. "Tell Dad good-bye for me."

"I will. Good-bye son."

"Bye." He placed the receiver back on the base and sat back in his chair.

"That was a close one," Rachel said.

Andrew looked at her evil smirk. "What do you mean?"

"You know exactly what I mean. You thought you were going to have to tell your mother that your daughter has Down syndrome. Why are you afraid to tell anyone?" Rachel asked.

"I'm not afraid," he said. "It's just that . . ."

"What?" Rachel pressed

"I can't explain it," Andrew said.

"You're not embarrassed are you?" she asked.

"Of course not," he said. "Why would I be embarrassed?"

Rachel shook her head and shrugged. "Just asking."

"It's not that I'm embarrassed. I guess I don't want to draw attention to it."

"I don't think informing your family could exactly be considered drawing attention to it," Rachel suggested.

"Well, it doesn't matter anyway. They'll all find out soon enough."

Rachel reached over and grasped Andrew's hand. "Could it be that you haven't accepted it yet?"

"What is there to accept? So she has Down syndrome. What's the big deal?"

"According to some of the reading I've done, a lot of people don't have a clear understanding of what it means. Some have the idea that these children should be institutionalized or that they can't be a benefit to society.'"

"I don't feel that way," Andrew said.

"I'm not suggesting you do, Andrew. But unless you figure out how you *do* feel, you won't know how to respond to those who have misconceptions."

Andrew nodded. "I guess I'm not . . . comfortable with it yet."

"Do you want to hold her?"

He looked down at Joy. "I hate to disturb a peaceful sleep," he said. "And speaking of sleeping, you were up most of the night—you must be tired."

"Now that you mention it, I guess I am," she admitted.

"I can put her in the bassinet if you'd like to get some sleep."

"Actually, I think I'd like to hold her for a while longer. The nurse said that would be okay."

"I'll let the two of you get some rest, and maybe I still have time to make it to the end of church," Andrew said.

"Okay," Rachel said with a smile.

Andrew stood and started to leave, but turned and went back to the bedside. He kissed the tip of his forefinger and touched it to the top of Joy's head. Then he leaned over and kissed Rachel. "I love you," he whispered.

Monday's echocardiogram revealed that there was no longer a hole between the chambers in Joy's heart. Since that had been the biggest health concern for the baby, Dr. Jeffery had agreed to release Joy on Tuesday with Rachel.

The couple met with the social worker right after lunch, and then Andrew went to the business office where he signed the discharge papers.

"Does she do anything but sleep?" Andrew asked sarcastically when he returned to the hospital room and found Rachel sitting on the bed with Joy sleeping in her arms.

The nurse chuckled. "Well, she eats occasionally, and believe me, once you get her home, you'll discover a few other things that she does on a regular basis."

Andrew laughed. "I can hardly wait."

"I guess we're ready," Rachel said.

"I'm required to take you to the car in this," the nurse said as she pushed a wheelchair over to the bedside.

"That's okay," Rachel said as she got into the wheelchair.

Andrew picked up Rachel's suitcase and a large bag of baby supplies the nurse had given her and followed the others to the car. Once outside, the nurse held Joy while Rachel got into the car, then she placed the baby in the infant seat and instructed Andrew in how to secure it properly. Rachel waved to the nurse as they drove from the parking lot.

"It's a beautiful afternoon," Rachel said as she looked around at the green lawns and blossoming late-summer flowers. "I know I've only been in the hospital for a few days, but it seemed a lot longer. It will be nice to be home again."

"It will be nice to have you there," Andrew said. "I'll bet you're looking forward to some real cooking after three days of hospital food."

"I don't know," she teased. "I've had your cooking before."

"Well, don't worry about that. Between your family

and the ladies at church, we'll have plenty of good cooking for the rest of the week."

"That's nice of everyone," she said. "Whose cooking do we have the pleasure of enjoying tonight?"

"It's a surprise."

"Why is it a surprise?"

"Because Edith made me promise . . . oops, I think I slipped," he said with a grin.

"That's so sweet of her. But don't worry, I'll act surprised."

Andrew smiled. "She felt bad about not being able to come see you at the hospital, so she insisted that she provide your first meal at home."

"Well, at least I know I can trust the cooking tonight."

Andrew nodded. "How do you think Edith will react when she sees Joy?"

"She'll be just fine. Why?"

"I was just thinking about what the social worker told us," he said. "It will be interesting to see if she is right about the way some people, especially those outside of the family, may react when they discover that Joy's a Down's baby."

"You know Edith will be fine with it," Rachel suggested. "But I am surprised she hasn't already asked you about it."

Andrew nodded. "Yeah, me too."

"She probably knew better," Rachel mumbled.

"What was that?" Andrew asked

"Nothing," Rachel replied.

The baby stirred as they drove to the end of their street and pulled into the driveway.

"She's probably hungry," Rachel said. "I guess I know what I'll be doing when I get inside."

Andrew opened the door for Rachel and helped her out of the car. "Why don't you get the baby, and I'll get the things out of the trunk," he said.

Rachel opened the back door and carefully lifted Joy from the infant seat while Andrew grabbed the suitcase from the trunk and hurried to beat them to the front door.

As Rachel entered the house, she stopped and took a deep breath, allowing the wonderful aroma to pass through her nostrils. "What is that delicious smell?"

A squeal of excitement could be heard in the kitchen, followed by a somewhat short, gray haired librarian rushing into the front room. "It's spaghetti sauce," Edith said. "My mother's secret recipe."

"It smells wonderful," Rachel said.

"Yes, it does," Andrew agreed. "When's dinner?"

"Not for a couple of hours," Edith said. "It still needs to simmer."

"I don't know if I can wait that long," Andrew complained.

"Oh, you'll wait," Edith teased as she looked over the top of her glasses and slapped the palm of her hand with the wooden spoon she was holding.

"I'll leave him to you while I go feed the baby," Rachel said.

"Oh, let me have a look at her first," Edith requested. She pulled the yellow receiving blanket down and stroked Joy's hand. "Isn't she precious? You two should be proud of yourselves."

"And she's such a good baby," Rachel volunteered. "I kept her in the hospital room with me most of the time, and she hardly ever cried. She just fussed a little when she needed to eat or be changed."

"Aren't those eyes beautiful?" Edith carefully touched

each closed eyelid. "Everyone has a distinguishing feature, and these eyes are certainly hers."

Rachel smiled and looked at Andrew. "Can't say that we'd thought about them that way, but it makes sense."

"Well, you'd better take care of that baby, Rachel. Andrew, I could use your help after you put that suitcase away."

"Yes, Mother," Andrew teased.

"I'll show you," Edith said as she playfully swatted the seat of Andrew's pants with her wooden spoon.

Rachel and Andrew had just sat down at the table when there was a knock at the door.

"I'll get it," Edith said as she walked to the front door and opened it. She just stood silently and stared at the man standing on the porch.

"I was hoping to see Andrew," the man said.

Edith stepped back and gestured for the stranger to step inside. "Please come in."

Andrew turned and looked up to see who the visitor was. He smiled broadly and left the table to greet his friend with a hand shake. "Come on in, Hank."

"I can see that I'm interrupting your dinner," Hank said as he entered the room. "I'll come back later."

"You're not interrupting," Andrew said. "In fact, I think we still owe you dinner, so why don't you join us?"

"I couldn't do that," he insisted.

"Why not?" Edith asked. "Are you afraid of my cooking?"

"No, ma'am," Hank said.

Andrew laughed. "Hank, this is our friend, Edith Huntington. Edith, this is Hank Peterman."

"I'm very pleased to meet you, Mr. Peterman. Now, are you joining us for dinner or not?"

Hank looked at Andrew, who just smiled and nodded. "Thank you, ma'am. That would be nice."

"I'll go get another place setting, but please, call me Edith."

"Yes ma'am . . . uh, Edith."

Andrew showed Hank to the dining area. "Hank, this is my wife, Rachel."

"It's a pleasure," Rachel said.

"Likewise," Hank replied. "I just came over to give you a little something." He held up a wrinkled paper bag and handed it to Rachel

Rachel opened the sack and pulled out a crocheted baby blanket. "This is beautiful, Hank."

"It's for the little one," he said.

"How did you know we were having a baby?" Andrew asked.

"I've seen your wife passing by," Hank said. "That's a hard thing to hide."

"Yeah, I guess it is," Andrew agreed. "But how did you know that she'd had the baby?"

"You left early Sunday morning, so I just figured," he said.

"You're full of surprises, aren't you?" Andrew muttered under his breath.

Edith returned with silverware and dishes for Hank. She placed them on the table and noticed the blanket on Rachel's lap. "Oh, isn't that beautiful," she gasped.

"Hank brought it for the baby," Rachel said.

"Where did you ever find such a beautiful blanket?" Edith asked.

Hank hesitated before answering. "My wife made it for our baby," he finally said.

chapter ✿ TWELVE

Andrew took his lunch from his briefcase and headed for the teacher's lounge. Lunchtime was nearly over, but he had been held up by a student who couldn't quite grasp the concept of polynomials. As he entered the lounge, two other teachers abruptly terminated their conversation.

"We were beginning to think you weren't going to make it," Jerry Tanner, the industrial arts teacher, said.

"I almost didn't," Andrew replied as he joined them at their table, unwrapped his tomato sandwich, and began eating. "I swear, that Williams boy may drive me to give up teaching," he said after swallowing.

Jerry laughed. "I had my turn last year."

"I guess I don't know this young man," Nancy Jensen said.

"Somehow, I don't think you'll have to worry about that, Nancy," Jerry chuckled. "This kid couldn't handle French if it was his native language."

"He's a nice enough kid," Andrew said.

"Yeah, he's nice, but sometimes I think he must be retar . . ." Jerry stopped mid-sentence, when Nancy kicked him under the table.

Andrew pretended not to notice his colleague's verbal misstep. "You're being too hard on him, Jerry."

"Maybe," Jerry admitted, rubbing his shin under the table.

"How are your wife and baby, Andrew?" Nancy asked in an attempt to change the direction of the conversation.

"They're fine," Andrew said, swallowing another bite of his sandwich.

"Wasn't she born just before school started?" Nancy asked.

He nodded. "Yeah, she's a little over two months old now."

"It must be hard," she said.

"What must be hard?" Andrew asked.

"Taking care of her," she said. "You know we really admire you."

"Thanks," Andrew said. "But for what?"

"What she means is that we think it's great how you're holding up so well under the circumstances," Jerry explained.

"What circumstances?" Andrew asked.

"You know—with your baby's . . . condition and everything," Nancy said.

Andrew shook his head. "I've got to go," he said as he took a bite of his apple and left the room.

Even though he tried not to, Andrew thought about

his brief conversation with Jerry and Nancy all afternoon. He wondered how they even knew that Joy had Down syndrome. He hadn't said anything to them, or to any of the other teachers.

Andrew stopped at the library on the way home. Edith was seated at her desk behind the front counter. "What does a guy have to do to get some service around here?" he teased.

Edith looked up over the top of her glasses and cocked her head to the side. "Hmm, let me think," she said. "I like chocolate."

"I'll remember that," Andrew promised.

"I prefer dark," Edith said as she stood up from her desk and walked to the counter.

"Busy day?" Andrew asked.

"Most days are now that school's back in session," she said. "How was your day?"

"So-so, I guess."

"That good, huh?" she asked.

"Oh, I guess I'm just letting people get to me," he said.

Edith just smiled and waited for Andrew to continue.

"A couple of teachers upset me a bit today."

"What did they do?" Edith asked.

"Maybe I'm making too much of it, but they asked about Joy as though she has some contagious disease."

"Did you correct them?"

Andrew shook his head. "No, I just ignored them."

"You probably should have corrected them," she suggested. "Their misconceptions will continue until someone does."

"You're probably right," Andrew agreed. "Anyway, I need to get home, but Rachel wanted me to confirm that you're still planning on joining us for Thanksgiving."

"I'll be there," Edith said. "And tell Rachel to let me know what I can bring."

"Okay," he said as he turned and left through the big glass door.

As he turned the corner onto his street, Andrew saw Hank just getting out of his pickup. He stopped and rolled down his window. "Hey, Hank," he called.

Hank turned and waved, then walked back to Andrew's car.

"You never answered me about Thanksgiving dinner," Andrew said. "Will you be joining us?"

Hank shrugged.

Andrew paused. "Hank, can I ask you something?"

"I guess," Hank said with little emotion.

"How long has it been since you've had a real Thanksgiving dinner?"

The flat expression on Hank's face didn't change as he thought for a moment. "Probably about fifty years," he said.

Andrew shook his head. "It's been too long, my friend. So how about it—will we see you there?"

"How big of a crowd is it going to be?" Hank questioned.

"Not too big," Andrew assured. "I just talked to Edith and she's coming for sure. So that would make the five of us, plus my parents and little sister."

Hank scratched his stubbly chin. "I guess that will be all right," he said.

Andrew couldn't hide the excitement in his broad smile. "Excellent!" he said. "I know Rachel will be delighted."

Hank put his hands in his pockets and nodded.

"Well, I'll see you later, then," Andrew said. He

rolled up the window and drove down the road to his own house.

Inside, Andrew found Rachel and Joy in the bathroom. Bath time was Joy's favorite time of day. Joy kicked and splashed just like any other child. Andrew just stood in the doorway and watched until Rachel noticed him.

"How long have you been home?" she asked.

"Not long," he answered.

"So how was school?"

"Okay, I guess," Andrew said.

"What's that supposed to mean?"

"Oh, nothing, really," he said.

"The kids are getting to you already?" Rachel teased.

"No . . . the teachers are."

Rachel's smile disappeared. "What happened?"

"Jerry and Nancy just frustrated me at lunch."

"How did they frustrate you?" Rachel asked as she lifted Joy from the tub and laid her on a towel.

"They said they knew it must be hard to care for Joy, and they admired me for handling it so well."

Rachel hesitated before responding. "You knew you'd get all kinds of responses from people."

"I know. But they thought I'd be offended just because Jerry almost called a student retarded?"

"I would be. That's not a very nice thing for a teacher to say about a student." Joy giggled as Rachel tickled under her arms with the towel.

Andrew chuckled. "I suppose you're right. Anyway, Nancy kicked him under the table before he could finish what he was saying."

"Serves him right," she said. "So what did you say?"

"Nothing. I just pretended that I hadn't noticed

and went on with the conversation."

Rachel shook her head. "You should have said something."

"Did Edith call and tell you to say that?" he asked.

"What?" Rachel asked.

Andrew shook his head. "I stopped at the library on the way home and Edith said the same thing."

"Smart woman," Rachel said as she fastened Joy's diaper and put her into her pajamas.

"I didn't know what to say to them," Andrew confessed.

"Well, until you figure that out, people will continue to say the same stupid things."

"It would be a whole lot easier if everyone reacted like our family has," he suggested.

"Yes, it would," Rachel agreed. "But you can't expect that to ever happen. A lot of people have never been exposed to Down's, so you can't really blame them for their ignorance."

"I guess," Andrew said.

"And, not everyone in the family reacted like you thought they should, either," Rachel said. "It took Mary at least a month to look at Joy a second time after she saw her at the hospital."

"Yeah, but that was more about Mary than Joy," Andrew said.

"Isn't that how it is for most people?" Rachel asked. "Aren't they all reacting to the disability rather than the child?"

"I guess you're right."

Rachel grinned. "I usually am." She lifted Joy, giving her a kiss on the forehead. "Come on, Joy, let's get you something to eat."

"Oh, that reminds me," Andrew said. "Edith confirmed

that she'll be here for Thanksgiving. And guess who else committed to come?"

"Hank?" Rachel asked.

"How did you know?"

Rachel rolled her eyes and smiled at her husband. "He's the only other person we'd invited that hasn't gotten back to us."

Andrew chuckled with embarrassment. "Oh, yeah."

"That ought to make Edith happy," Rachel said as she walked to the front room and sat in the rocking chair.

Andrew nodded in agreement as he followed his wife to the front of the house. "That's exactly what I thought."

"It's kind of ironic, don't you think?" Rachel asked.

"What? That Edith seems particularly friendly to Hank lately?" Andrew asked.

"No. That just a few months ago you two were on the hunt for clues that proved he was a murderer," Rachel said.

"Okay, but you do have to admit that she seems quick to defend him lately."

Rachel nodded. "Don't you agree that he seems too nice to be a killer?"

"I agree," Andrew said. "In any case, I'd still like to know what really happened in that house."

"I didn't think I'd ever say this, but I'm kind of curious myself," Rachel admitted. "We may never know."

"Someday we'll know," Andrew said confidently. He picked up the newspaper and began reading.

After she finished feeding the baby, Rachel laid Joy's head on her shoulder and gently patted her back. "Do you want to put her in bed after I finish burping her?" she asked.

Andrew opened his mouth to answer when the

telephone rang. "I'll get that," he said as he stood and left the room.

Rachel got up early to put the turkey in the oven and begin preparing for Thanksgiving dinner. She and Andrew had peeled potatoes the night before, so most of the hard work was done—especially since Edith and Sandra were bringing the pies, rolls, and yams.

Andrew heard the commotion coming from the kitchen and after twenty minutes or so, decided to see if he could help. "Anything I can do?" he asked as he staggered into the kitchen.

Rachel smiled and puckered her lips.

"Anything else?" Andrew said after giving her a kiss.

"Not at this point, but maybe once your parents are here," she said. "What time were they expecting to arrive?"

"Dad said they planned to leave around five, so they should get here around eight I would think."

"Wow. That early?" Rachel asked.

"Mom said she wants plenty of time with Joy," Andrew said.

Rachel nodded. "Joy will be waking soon, so maybe I'll try and get these dishes washed before I have to tend to her. You can go back to bed for another half hour if you want."

"Are you sure?" he asked.

"I'm sure. I'll get you up at seven-thirty."

Andrew hadn't gotten very far when Joy began to

fuss. He turned and went back to the kitchen. "I have a better idea," he said. "Why don't I do the dishes?"

Rachel took off her apron and handed it to Andrew. "Thank you," she said with a chuckle. "Guess we'll see you in a little while." She entered the bedroom and took the baby from the bassinet and laid her on the bed. After changing Joy's diaper, Rachel began the feeding ritual.

Rachel had read that some babies with Down syndrome had a difficult time breast feeding, but Joy was doing quite well. She took longer to eat than the average baby, which Rachel found frustrating at first. Eventually, she had come to enjoy the extra time it gave her to bond with her little girl. "You're so precious," Rachel said as she stroked Joy's head.

Joy stopped eating momentarily as she turned her head and looked up at her mother, but quickly resumed her position and continued with the task at hand.

Rachel smiled as she thought about the past three months since Joy's birth. Because this was her first child, she had nothing to compare her experience to. Much to her surprise, she was finding that, in many ways, it was not as hard as she had expected. Joy seemed to be developing at nearly the same rate as other babies her age, which, according to Joy's social worker, was normal. Rachel and Andrew had been told that Joy's developmental delays would begin at about six months, so perhaps things would become more challenging. Either way, Rachel enjoyed being a mother.

Andrew finished the dishes and joined the girls in the bedroom. "I suppose I'd just as well get dressed now," he said.

"Yep," Rachael agreed. "Your parents will be here soon."

"It will be good to see them again," Andrew said as he put on a pair of jeans.

"Yes it will," Rachel said. "I'm sure they must be excited to see their first grandchild."

Andrew buttoned his shirt and began tying his shoes. "Do you think so?" he asked sarcastically. "Just because Mom calls every week for a progress report doesn't mean she's excited."

Rachel laughed. "She probably knows more about Joy than my mother and Mom sees Joy at least once a week."

"But Joy's not your mother's first grandchild."

"That's true," Rachel acknowledged.

"I guess I'll leave you two while I go set up the table," Andrew said. He left the bedroom and went outside to the old garage. He had borrowed a large banquet table from James and Elizabeth. The old table had folding legs and was leaning against the side wall. Andrew hoped he could manage to haul it inside by himself, since both he and James had lifted it together when James delivered it. As he stood, staring at the table, the sound of a car caught his attention. He turned around and waved as his parent's car stopped in front of the house.

Rushing over to greet his visitors, Andrew opened the front passenger door and assisted his mother out of the car. He wrapped his arm around Sandra and squeezed tightly.

"It's wonderful to see you, son," she said. "Where's the baby?"

Andrew chuckled. "It's good to see you too, Mom. She's inside with Rachel."

Rob and Brenda got out of the car and joined the others. Andrew gave them both a hug.

"Let's get inside before Mom bursts," Andrew suggested.

"You guys go ahead," Brenda said. "I'll bring the food in." She had returned to college a few weeks after Joy was born and had visited Rachel and Andrew several times since then.

"I'll help," Andrew offered.

"Don't worry about it," Brenda said. "There's only a couple of things. I can get them."

Andrew nodded and led his parents to the front porch.

"This looks like a lovely home," Sandra said. "Are you enjoying it here?"

"We've really liked it here," Andrew assured.

"You don't have many neighbors. Do you feel isolated?" Rob asked.

"Not really," Andrew said. "We're just a block away from a larger neighborhood, and it's nice not to be sandwiched between a bunch of houses in a subdivision. That's why we chose this old place."

"You two can visit if you want," Sandra said as she opened the front door. "I'm going inside to see my granddaughter."

Rob chuckled. "Just the one neighbor then?" he asked as he pointed in the general direction of Hank's house.

"That's it," Andrew said. "He's a really nice guy—in fact, he's joining us today, so you'll get to meet him."

Brenda came up the sidewalk and joined her father and brother.

"Let me get that for you," Andrew offered as he held open the screen door for his sister.

When they all went inside, they found Sandra in the rocking chair, beaming over Joy. Rachel was seated on the sofa.

"I see you found her," Rob said as he walked over and knelt beside the rocking chair. He gently touched Joy's hand. A proud smile swept over his face when the baby took hold of his finger. "What a beautiful child," he said softly. "You should both be mighty proud."

After Andrew and Rob put the banquet table in the front room and placed folding chairs around it, the ladies placed a tablecloth on it and decorated it with Thanksgiving centerpieces.

Edith, who had arrived a couple of hours after Andrew's parents, was busy arranging the place settings on the table.

Brenda came from the kitchen with a nicely browned turkey on a platter and placed it on the end of the table. Rachel followed behind her with a large carving knife. "The turkey's ready for carving," she announced. "As soon as Hank arrives, we can eat."

Andrew looked at his watch. "I told him we'd be eating at noon."

"He's a nice man, but he's not worth cold turkey and dressing. Either you go get him or I will," Edith said to Andrew.

"I'll be right back," Andrew said as he stood and left through the front door.

"Couldn't you have just called him?" Rob asked.

"He's a little old fashioned," Edith said. "No telephone."

Outside, Andrew hurried down the road to Hank's house and knocked on the front door.

"Door's open," Hank yelled from inside.

In spite of their contact with each other over the past

several months, Andrew had never been inside Hank's house. He took hold of the doorknob and turned as he pushed on the door, but it didn't budge. Taking a cue from earlier experiences, he lowered his shoulder and threw it against the solid oak slab. The door swung open and Andrew stepped inside. "It's just me, Hank."

"Won't be a minute," Hank called from another room.

Andrew looked around at his surroundings. Directly in front of him was a large mirror on the wall, covered with the same haze that coated all the other glass in the room. Against the same wall, a little to the right, was an old wood burning stove. An old sofa was centered against the wall to his right and under the big front window was a drop-leaf table with a dingy tablecloth. In the center of the table was a bowl of plastic fruit, covered in thick dust and cobwebs.

Leaning forward a little, Andrew could see into the kitchen. Though he could see little of the room itself, there was a small chrome-legged table and two matching chairs in view. He noticed that the linoleum on the floor had a path worn in it down to bare wood. Andrew followed the path with his eyes and discovered that it extended to the carpet in the room where he was standing. Although the entire carpet appeared to have had a great deal of wear, there was a definite path worn from the kitchen to a platform rocker and from there to a doorway that led into a dark hall.

Andrew was startled by the sound of footsteps approaching from the hall.

"Sorry," Hank said. "I'm running a bit behind schedule. Had some problems at the farm."

"No prob . . ." Andrew stared at Hank as he emerged from the darkness of the hallway.

"Should we go?" Hank asked.

Andrew nodded, slowly. Instead of the usual bib over-alls, Hank was dressed in a pair of gray slacks and a white shirt. It took Andrew a second to figure out what else was different, but then he noticed the stubble-free face. "Hank, you look great."

Hank shrugged and headed for the front door. He left the door open for Andrew as he proceeded toward the Ingram house.

"My parents are looking forward to meeting you," Andrew said as he caught up to Hank.

Hank continued without saying a word.

Once they arrived at Andrew's house, Andrew introduced Hank to his parents and sister. Then everyone joined at the table and bowed their heads as Rachel gave thanks for the food they were about to eat and the bless-ing of being together.

Rob was given the honor of carving the turkey, and Thanksgiving dinner began. Everyone enjoyed plenty of good food and friendly conversation. The afternoon was made complete when Edith brought out a variety of home-made pies and allowed everyone to help themselves.

"It's custom in my house that everyone helps with the Thanksgiving dishes," Edith announced once every-one had finished eating.

"Hey, wait a minute," Andrew complained. "You live alone."

"That's right," Edith said, "and everyone helps with the dishes."

"I like that custom," Rachel said.

The women laughed as the three men looked at each other and began clearing the table.

When all the dishes were washed and put away, everyone gathered in the front room. They brought a couple of folding chairs from the dinner table so everyone had a place to sit and visit while dinner digested.

"Andrew," Rachel said. "It sounds like Joy's awake. Will you go get her?"

Andrew looked at Edith. "I'll bet Edith would like to get her," he suggested.

"I'd love to," Edith said hesitantly. She stood and went to the bedroom for the baby.

Rachel sighed heavily as Edith left the room.

When Edith returned with Joy, Sandra broke the silence. "Edith, I don't know when I've tasted better pie," she said.

"My mother taught me to bake," Edith replied. "It's not very often that I have the chance to cook for a crowd, so this has been a real treat for me."

"Andrew and Rachel, we want to thank you for hosting all of us," Rob added. "We hope it's not been too much work with the new baby and all."

"I have to admit, I was a bit nervous. With everyone's help, though, I've really enjoyed it," Rachel said.

"Why would you be nervous?" Edith asked.

"I don't know," Rachel admitted. "It's just that I've always had Thanksgiving dinner at my mother's, so I haven't been too involved with planning or anything in the past. It was easy to bring one item, but I wasn't sure how I'd handle organizing the whole event."

Sandra winked at Rachel. "You've handled it beautifully."

"What did you think, Hank?" Rob asked.

"Very nice," Hank said.

"Have you ever had a better meal?" Rob continued.

Hank shook his head.

Rob had noticed that Hank said very little during dinner, so he wanted to involve him in a conversation.

"So what do you do for a living?" he asked.

"Farmer," Hank replied.

"What kind of farm?" Rob questioned.

"Cattle and hay," Hank said.

Rob nodded. "Do you sell your hay, or just grow enough for your cattle?"

"Just for my stock," Hank answered.

"How many cattle do you have?" Andrew asked.

"About a hundred head at the moment." Hank didn't seem interested in volunteering any information, though it didn't seem to bother him to answer the questions.

"Do you enjoy it?" Rob asked.

Hank nodded. "I suppose so."

Finally, Edith stood and walked over to where Hank was sitting. "Have you ever seen such a beautiful baby?" she asked as she knelt down with Joy in her arms.

Hank didn't say anything, but looked around the room at the others.

"Isn't she the most beautiful baby you've ever seen?" Edith repeated. "Would you like to hold her?"

"Some other time," Hank said with obvious discomfort.

"You said once that you had a baby," Edith continued. "I guess I can't blame you if you think your own baby was more beautiful."

Hank shook his head. "Didn't get a chance to find out," he said.

"Edith," Andrew whispered in embarrassment for his friend.

Ignoring Andrew, Edith persisted in questioning Hank. "I'm sorry to hear that, Hank. What happened?"

Hank's face turned red and he started breathing faster. "The baby died," he said.

"It must be very difficult to lose a baby. I'm sorry if

I got too personal," Edith apologized.

"It's okay," Hank said as he cleared his throat.

"You'd probably give anything to hold your own baby in your arms right now, wouldn't you, Hank?" Edith asked.

Hank nodded.

"It's sad to think that some fathers don't take advantage of that opportunity when they have it," Edith said as she looked at Andrew.

chapter ❀ THIRTEEN

"Merry Christmas!" everyone shouted as Rachel, Andrew, and Joy left Martha's house and headed home after a delightful evening with Rachel's family for the annual Cooper family Christmas Eve celebration.

Andrew took Rachel's arm and helped her navigate the snowy sidewalk. He opened the back door of the car.

"Can you believe it was just last year that we thought we would be spending Christmas without Mom?" Rachel asked as she strapped Joy into the infant seat.

Andrew opened the front passenger door for Rachel once Joy was secure. "It does seem like it was a long time ago," he said.

"I suppose that's because so much has happened this

year," Rachel suggested when Andrew climbed behind the wheel and backed out of the driveway.

Andrew nodded.

Rachel smiled as she looked through the windshield at the light snow that was falling. Each flake appeared particularly large as it was caught in the car headlights. "Isn't it beautiful?" she asked.

Andrew nodded again.

"This is just how Christmas Eve should be," Rachel said. She looked at Andrew, who seemed to be off in his own wonderland. "What're you thinking about?" she asked.

Andrew shook his head. "Nothing really."

"Right."

"Well, nothing important," Andrew said. "I'm just thinking about what it will be like tomorrow—you know, Christmas day as a family."

"I'm looking forward to our first Christmas with Joy too."

"I'd like to think we've had joy in all our Christmases," Andrew said with a smile.

Rachel gently slapped Andrew's leg. "You know what I mean."

Andrew laughed. "Yes, I know what you mean. I was thinking of this being our first Christmas with the baby, but I was thinking about the others too. It's kind of like our little family of two has suddenly grown to a family of five."

"You mean with Edith and Hank?" Rachel asked. "We're just fortunate to have these three wonderful people enter our lives."

"And one of them still has me baffled," Andrew said. "No matter how hard I try, I can't figure out who or what he is."

"You just can't let it go, can you?" Rachel said. "We may not know Hank very well, but you've spent time with him and we've even had him in our home. How can you still think he might be a killer?"

"I know, but . . . ."

"No buts," Rachel said. "Didn't you see the look on his face when he gave us that blanket for Joy?"

"But how do you explain the newspaper article? That stuff wasn't just made up," Andrew argued.

"I don't know," Rachel admitted. "But I'm sure there's a reasonable explanation."

"Hank certainly doesn't seem interested in sharing it with anyone. Doesn't that make you wonder?"

Rachel considered Andrew's argument as they approached their street and rounded the corner. She stared at Hank's house as they passed. "How do you know he won't share it? Have you ever asked him directly?" she asked.

Andrew shook the head. "You read the article. He said he killed them, but then refused to say anything else," Andrew said as he pulled the car into the driveway.

"He said he was sorry," Rachel pointed out.

"So that makes it all right?"

Rachel released her seat belt and turned so she was facing Andrew. "No, it doesn't make it all right, but it makes me even more convinced that there's an explanation for what happened."

Andrew sighed heavily. "I sure hope there is. But I still wonder why he hasn't said anything by now."

"Maybe he will."

Andrew shook his head. "Didn't we just go through this?"

"Maybe no one has asked the right questions."

"What do you mean—what are the right questions?"

"You know as well as I do that Hank is a man of few words," she said.

"So!"

"He rarely volunteers any information," she continued.

"Are you suggesting that the sheriff and everyone else back then were too stupid to ask the right questions?"

"I'm suggesting that the right questions, asked in the right way by the right person, might get the right answers." Rachel paused. "It makes sense, doesn't it?" Rachel asked.

Andrew considered his wife's hypothesis. "You think that Hank would be more responsive if someone he knows and trusts were to pick the right moment to ask him about the incident."

"Exactly," Rachel said.

"Well, I guess I'll start watching for that moment when he joins us tomorrow," Andrew said.

Rachel smiled at her well intentioned husband and gently placed her hand on his knee. "No offense, but I was thinking of Edith as the right person."

Andrew blushed slightly. "Well, I guess that does make more sense."

"Come on, we'd better go inside. We need to get the house ready for tomorrow."

Snow continued falling through the night, leaving a fresh white blanket about two inches thick. Andrew went outside and shoveled the sidewalks while Rachel tended to Joy. Inside, he plugged in the Christmas tree lights and built a fire in the fireplace.

"What a great idea," Rachel said as she entered the room with Joy in her arms. "It's been awhile since we've had a fire."

"Yeah, I thought it was about time," Andrew said.

"We'd better get breakfast. Then we can have things cleaned up and ready for our guests," Rachel suggested.

"Can we eat in front of the fire?" Andrew asked.

Rachel smiled. "I guess it won't hurt this morning."

"Great," Andrew said. "I'll go get everything." He hurried to the kitchen and soon returned with all the necessary ingredients for their traditional Christmas breakfast: a box of their favorite cold cereal, a carton of milk, a carton of eggnog, two bowls, two spoons, and two glasses.

"The breakfast of champions," Rachel said.

Andrew grinned. "Isn't it great?"

Rachel smiled and shook her head. "Remind me why we do this."

"Because it's quick, easy, and Christmassy," Andrew replied.

"Right—Christmassy," Rachel repeated as she sat Joy on the floor between two pillows.

Joy had matured to the point that she could remain sitting up if she was propped with something support-ing her on the sides. Though still unable to roll over on her own, she had recently discovered that she could fall over from the propped-up sitting position if she leaned far enough forward. Her parents would laugh as they rolled her onto her back or sat her back up and she would grin and giggle along with them.

"Well, that was ... breakfast. Thank you, honey," Rachel said with a wink as she finished her bowl of cereal.

"I'll clear these dishes. Then I'll go pick up Edith," Andrew said.

"I was wondering if it would be all right if I picked up Edith while you did the dishes," Rachel said.

"Why?" Andrew asked.

"I just thought it would give you a chance to bond with Joy," she replied. "You do realize that you've never been alone with her since she was born?"

"I guess I hadn't thought about it," he said. "Anyway, the roads are snowy."

"It's only a couple of inches. What's the matter? Don't you trust my driving?" Rachel gathered the dishes and put them on the tray Andrew had used to bring them in.

"I trust your driving. It's just that . . . well, you know I worry about you driving alone."

Rachel knew she had to think quickly in order to convince Andrew that she could go get Edith. "So you'd rather that I was here alone with Hank? He'll be arriving in a few minutes."

"Now what am I supposed to say?" Andrew asked.

"That you'll let me go get Edith," she answered.

Andrew nodded. "Okay, you can go get her."

Rachel kissed Andrew on the cheek as she left to take the tray of dishes to the kitchen. She returned from the bedroom with her purse and coat. "I won't be long," she said as she kissed Andrew again.

"I've already scraped the snow off the car," Andrew said.

"Thank you," Rachel called over her shoulder as she left through the front door.

Rachel loved making the first tracks in freshly fallen snow. As she drove up the road and turned the corner, she noticed Hank through her rearview mirror as he left his house and headed to hers.

A thin layer of high clouds prevented the sun from being visible, but with the new snow, everything was still bright. Rachel didn't see any other people or cars as she drove to Edith's house. She backed into the driveway, which had been cleared of snow, as had the sidewalks.

Just for fun, Rachel stopped on her way to the front door and made a snowball. She smiled with youthful pleasure as she threw it into the middle of the street then knocked on the door. "You've been busy," Rachel said when Edith opened her front door.

Edith looked surprised. "I have?"

Rachel turned and looked at the driveway.

"That wasn't me. It was my thoughtful neighbors," Edith explained. "Anyway, looks like you pulled it off."

"Yeah, but it wasn't easy," Rachel said.

"How'd you get him to let you come?" Edith asked.

Rachel smiled. "I just asked him if he'd be more comfortable with me at home with Hank or driving in the snow."

Edith giggled. "Good girl. Well I'm ready, so I'll meet you in the garage."

"Okay," Rachel said. She returned to the car and waited for the garage door to open, then backed the car inside. She got out and opened the trunk.

Edith laid her bag on the front seat of the car. Then she went back by Rachel. "Let's do it."

The two ladies each took hold of one side of a large box sitting on the floor and lifted it into the trunk.

"I hope he likes it," Rachel said.

"He's a man, and it's a tool," Edith teased. "Of course he'll like it."

Rachel laughed. "We'd better get going, or he'll start to worry."

"You pull forward and I'll close the garage door," Edith instructed.

Rachel complied with Edith's directive and waited as Edith secured the garage and climbed into the front seat.

"You got a two-for-one deal out of this, didn't you Rachel?"

"How do you mean?" Rachel asked as she pulled from the driveway.

"You were able to get Andrew's gift without him knowing it, and you forced him to be alone with the baby," Edith explained.

Rachel gave a non-convincing nod. "I'm not sure it will do any good. He'll only have her for a few minutes, and she'll probably still be sitting where she was when I left her."

"Well, it's a start," Edith suggested. "Has he held her at all?"

"He'll pick her up and hand her to me. He'll even change her diaper, but he won't hold her for longer than that."

Edith sat in silence for a few minutes as they drove. Finally she spoke. "He'll come around when the time is right for him."

"Speaking of the right time," Rachel said, "Andrew and I were talking last night, and we think we know a way to find out what really happened at the Peterman's."

"You do?" Edith asked in surprise.

"We think that if someone he trusts asks at the right time, he may open up." She turned and looked briefly at Edith. "I'll bet he trusts you."

"What makes you say that?" Edith asked.

"Do I need to remind you about Thanksgiving and how far you pushed Hank?" Rachel asked.

"That was more for Andrew than Hank," Edith said.

"I know, but he answered every one of your questions," Rachel said.

"I guess he did," Edith acknowledged. "I wonder why?"

"You're not serious, are you?" Rachel asked.

Edith looked confused.

"Edith, I think Hank likes you."

"Oh, don't be ridiculous. I'm an old lady," Edith said.

"Hank's no young buck himself," Rachel argued. "But what's age got to do with it anyway?"

"Well," Edith stammered. "What if he does like me? Those kinds of feelings have to go two ways."

Rachel chuckled. "I think they do."

Edith blushed. "What are you implying?"

"Nothing," Rachel assured. "Anyway, are you willing to help us solve this mystery?"

"I suppose," Edith answered as they turned the corner onto Rachel's street.

Rachel pulled the car into the driveway. "We can leave the saw in the trunk for now. I'm giving him an envelope with a picture of it from the catalog."

"That'll keep him guessing," Edith said with a smile.

The two ladies went into the house and joined the others. Hank had arrived and was sitting on the hearth, staring into the fire. Once again, he was nicely dressed in his gray pants and white shirt.

Andrew was seated on the sofa, next to Joy, who was right where Rachel had left her.

"Merry Christmas, all!" Edith shouted as she took off her coat and handed it to Rachel.

"Merry Christmas," Andrew said.

Hank gave a quick nod. "Ma'am."

"Is that the best you two can do?" Edith asked.

Andrew laughed as he stood and gave Edith a hug.

"That's more like it," she said. "Hank, how are things with you?"

"Fine, thank you," he replied.

Edith knelt in front of Joy. "How's my little sweetie?"

Joy giggled as Edith tickled the bottom of her feet.

"I think we're ready to get started here," Rachel said as she came into the room. She put on the sweater she had brought with her and sat on the sofa with Joy next to her feet.

"We just thought we'd exchange a few gifts. Then we can visit while the ham cooks," Andrew said.

"In other words, the men will visit while the women prepare dinner," Edith said with a wink.

"We'll help," Andrew said.

"You guys are just lucky it's a simple meal," Rachel teased.

Andrew laughed as he took a gift from under the tree. "Look, Joy, this one's for you," he said as he handed the present to her.

Joy swatted at the gift a bit, but showed little interest.

"May I help her?" Edith asked.

Rachel nodded her approval.

Edith opened the package to reveal a soft, colorful cloth ball. She put the toy in Joy's hand.

Everyone laughed as Joy squeezed the ball a few times and then dropped it to play with the wrapping paper instead. They open her other gifts and put them next to her to enjoy if she ever chose to give up the paper.

Rachel and Andrew gave a few small gifts to Edith and Hank and exchanged their gifts to each other. Rachel was delighted with her new sewing machine, and Andrew was elated with the new addition to his workshop.

Edith gave Rachel and Andrew a lovely table clock and Joy a musical rattle. She surprised Hank with a tie to match his pants.

Without saying anything, Hank opened a bag on the floor next to him and gave a gift to everyone in the room. To Rachel, he gave a variety of hand lotions and soaps; Andrew received a set of socket wrenches. He shocked Edith with a beautiful handkerchief, and he presented Joy with a handmade baby quilt.

"Where did you find something like this?" Edith asked as she looked at her beautiful handkerchief with a hand tatted border.

"My wife made it," was his matter-of-fact reply.

Rachel was looking at the detail in the quilt. "Did she make this as well?"

"She did," he answered.

"Hank," Edith began, "excuse me if I'm being too nosy, but . . . ." She hesitated for a moment. Then she took a deep breath and continued. "You haven't told us much about your wife. She was obviously a very talented woman."

Hank responded with the usual silent nod.

"We'd like to know more about her," Edith said.

"I don't really like to talk about it," he responded.

"We don't mean to press, Hank. But we're your friends," Rachel interjected.

"I know you are," Hank said. "Better friends than I deserve."

"What makes you say that?" Andrew asked. "We all consider you a good friend."

Hank looked up at Edith. "You've lived here all your life. I'm sure you know who I am."

Edith remained silent so Hank could continue.

After a few moments, he looked down at the floor. "Many years ago, I did a very bad thing, for which I'm very sorry. But sorry doesn't undo the damage."

"Everyone makes mistakes," Edith said.

"But everyone doesn't kill their wife and child," he returned.

Rachel gasped as she put her hand over her mouth. "I can't believe that, Hank."

He continued staring at the floor, but didn't speak.

"We've heard rumors, but we don't believe them," Edith said.

Hank sighed. "It was August, and I was busy trying to get in a late crop of hay. Doris wasn't due for several weeks but had started having contractions. We were both scared, and I offered to stay home that day. She knew how much we'd struggled that summer and that this crop was crucial. I was trying to beat a storm that was on its way, so she insisted that she would be all right. I came home and checked on her at lunchtime, and the contractions were getting harder. I told her I'd stay with her, but she insisted that she was okay. So, against my better judgment, I returned to the farm."

Everyone waited silently when he stopped speaking.

With tears forming in his eyes, Hank continued. "I remember sitting on the tractor and having the feeling that I should go check on Doris. But the clouds were rolling in, and I was almost done baling that field, so I kept working. I had a bad feeling, but I ignored it. Then . . . ." He paused as he wiped his eyes. "When I finally did go home, I found her and the baby dead on the floor in a pool of blood." He put his face into his hands. "I didn't mean to kill them, I really didn't," he kept repeating.

Edith and Rachel each moved to sit on either side of

Hank and each put an arm around his shoulder.

"You didn't kill them, Hank," Edith said softly. "It wasn't your fault."

"I should have acted on my feelings," he said between sniffles.

"Hank, you didn't kill them," Rachel repeated. "You didn't cause their deaths."

"But I could have prevented them," he argued.

"You don't know that," Edith said.

Hank just shook his head. "Yes I do," he whispered.

Edith pulled him a little closer. "Hank, you didn't kill them," she repeated.

"You're probably the only ones that believe that," he said.

Andrew cleared his throat. "I just have to ask," he said timidly. "Why didn't you tell your story to the sheriff? It seems that you could have cleared up this whole mess back then if you'd told him what you've just shared with us."

Hank looked up at Andrew. "This isn't about what the law or what anyone else thinks; this is about what I did," he said sternly. "I knew I could tell my story and make everyone feel sorry for me, but that would have made it too easy for me to forget what an awful thing I had done. Justifying it won't bring them back."

"It seems to me, Hank, that you've been suffering needlessly all these years," Andrew said. "I don't mean to be insensitive," he continued, "but I bet that you don't even remember any of the good times with your wife because you're so weighed down by something that wasn't even your fault. The last fifty years could have been filled with joy, if you'd only accepted things the way they were, and moved forward."

"You make it sound so easy," Hank disputed.

Andrew shook his head. "I'm not suggesting that you forget, Hank; only that you be grateful for what you have and make the best of it."

"Haven't you been listening to me?" Hank said in frustration. "I sacrificed my family for a field of hay."

"How do you know things would have been any different if you'd stayed with Doris?" Edith asked. "Maybe she wouldn't have let you take her to the doctor, even if you'd been there."

"I guess we'll never know," Hank said quietly as he lowered his head.

No one knew how to respond, so Edith finally spoke up. "What can we do to help, Hank?" she asked, even though she knew what the answer was likely to be.

"There's nothing anyone can do," Hank insisted.

Rachel had been thinking about something Hank had said earlier. "Hank, did you say this happened in August?"

Hank nodded.

"What day in August?"

He shook his head. "I don't remember for sure."

Andrew suddenly understood why Rachel was questioning Hank. "I'll be right back," he said as he left the room. Andrew quickly returned with a piece of paper in his hand. "August 26th," he said.

"Could have been," Hank responded.

"It was August 26th," Andrew confirmed. "It's right here in this newspaper article."

Hank shifted his gaze from the floor to Andrew. "Okay, it was August 26th," he said.

"That's the day Joy was born," Rachel said softly.

Hank took in a deep breath and exhaled slowly as he nodded, but remained silent.

"You knew, didn't you?" Edith asked.

Hank looked up at Edith and nodded.

"And that's why you brought Joy the crocheted blanket," Rachel said.

"I guess I hoped it would help somehow," Hank admitted.

"Did it?" Andrew asked.

Hank bowed his head as he thought about how to respond. "I figured that being around your baby could fill some of that empty void in my heart."

Rachel motioned for Andrew to bring her the baby.

Andrew went to where Joy was contentedly playing with Christmas wrapping paper and picked her up. He returned to the hearth and handed Joy to Rachel.

Rachel turned to Hank. "Is this close enough?" she asked as she placed Joy in Hank's arms. "We hope you will accept her as your honorary granddaughter."

Hank gratefully took Joy into his arms. "I will," he promised. "I will."

Rachel looked at Andrew, who smiled and nodded his approval.

"Who would have thought that a little baby could bring joy where there had only been sadness?" Hank asked.

"God obviously knew one could," Edith said quietly. "After all, isn't that what today's all about?"

Everyone nodded as they reflected on the meaning of the day that brought them together.

Hank's eyes began to mist again as he looked at little Joy in his arms and felt the love of those around him. "If I only knew that Doris didn't blame me," he said somberly.

Something prompted Rachel to look across the room. She tapped Edith's shoulder and gestured for her and Andrew to look to the other side of the room.

Andrew's eyes grew wide and his jaw dropped as he stared into the distance.

"Hank," Edith whispered.

Hank lifted his head and looked at Edith.

Edith shook her head and pointed.

Hank turned his eyes to where Edith was pointing. Tears streamed down his face as he gazed at the image of his wife, holding a baby in her arms and smiling. "Doris," he said softly—and the image disappeared.

No one spoke as Hank wept. He pulled Joy closer to his chest and gently rocked back and forth. After several minutes, he wiped his eyes with his hands and looked at Andrew.

"It's your turn," Hank said.

Andrew looked perplexed. "My turn for what?" he asked.

Hank looked deep into Andrew's eyes, then down at Joy, but said nothing.

Andrew's confusion was replaced with understanding as his eyes were drawn to his little girl.

"Take your own advice," Hank said with a grin. "Fill your life with joy by accepting things as they are and moving forward."

Andrew reached for his daughter. He pulled her close to his chest and kissed the top of her head. "You're right," he said. "I can fill my life with Joy."

Hank smiled at Rachel and put his arm around Edith's shoulder. "Merry Christmas, Edith," he said with a smile.

Rachel's eyes began to tear. She reached into the pocket of her sweater for a tissue, but couldn't find one. Instead she found a small, folded slip of paper. She opened the paper and smiled as she read what was written on it. "Oh my," she said.

"What do you have there?" Edith asked.

Rachel handed Edith the paper that had come from a fortune cookie many months before.

Edith read it aloud. "True happiness comes from accepting joy."

about the author

Todd F. Cope grew up in Spanish Fork, Utah. After graduating from high school, he served an LDS mission to Australia, where he met a missionary from New Zealand who later became his wife. Todd and Denise were married in New Zealand and lived there for two years before moving to the United States. Today they reside in Spanish Fork with their four children.

Todd graduated from Utah Valley State College with an associate's degree in nursing and later from Weber State University with a bachelor's degree in nursing. He works as the director of nursing at an assisted living center in Provo, Utah.

Todd is the author of *So Much for Christmas, A Dream Come True*, and *The Shift*, a self-published novel that inspired the CBS television movie *The Last Dance*, starring Maurine O'Hara.